To

Baba and Mam.

To

DF, GW, DK, LK, NS, SN.

for Asim

ar.

CHAPTER 1

It was a beautiful autumn day. The morning sun shone through the maple trees into Marina's room. She was still wearing her nightgown. The milk-laden coffee she had brought upstairs was now cold. She looked at the clock for the sixth time in as many minutes, and as soon as it struck seven, picked up the phone and slowly dialled the number.

"Hello, Aunti. This is Marina. Is Sabina there?"

"Yes, of course. Is everything all right?"

"Yes, Aunti. Everything is fine. Could you please call Sabina."

"Hello, Marina. What's up?" Sabina sounded as if she had just woken up.

"Sabina, what are you doing today?"

"Nothing special."

"Could you come over?"

"Yes, but why?"

"My engagement day is set."

***

Colonel Javed looked at the neatly-hung three-piece suit and the elegant *shalwar-kameez* dress with its knee-long shirt and baggy trousers. Once again, he wondered which to wear on his daughter's engagement day. He thought about his relatives from the village who would be arriving around noon. All would be dressed in the traditional *shalwar-kameez*. There were so many questions he would like to ask Uncle Sherdil. How are the crops doing? Is the water supply good? Was the bathroom wall repaired? His pulse rose when he thought about how Uncle Sherdil would narrate reactions to what Javed had earlier said about cousin Fakir's son. Why Javed would not marry his daughter to that illiterate good for nothing bum. It was fun to talk to Uncle Sherdil, especially about village gossip. Uncle always knew what Javed wanted to hear and would say it with such skill. Ah, to hear his native Pashto language. The nuances, the intonation, the key words. None of these city languages could be as exciting.

City. Javed raised his eyebrows. General Beg. He would be coming to the ceremony this evening. It was so obvious. He must wear the suit and tie. How else could he receive the General. Not in a *shalwar-kameez*. He couldn't recall ever seeing the General in traditional apparel. And Colonel Ashiq and Colonel Imtiaz. All would be there. Javed smiled. And to think this decision had been so difficult last night.

***

The colourful tent canopy rested on thick bamboo supports connected to ropes pegged into the lawn of Colonel Javed's beautiful mansion. The uncomfortable orange plastic chairs were arranged along the four walls of the tent. Large bright bulbs shone with light as the evening festivities passed into the night. At one side of the enclosure, on a platform, was a brightly decorated three-piece sofa set. Marina sat here with her fiancé, Adil. Family members kept coming to the stage, sitting on either side of the couple for the all-important photographs. Marina and Adil occupied themselves by talking to their guests, hardly a word between themselves. Children of all sizes ran about displaying the widest variety of dress code. Flower petals lay on the path the couple had taken from the house to the platform.

The music turned to a popular tune. Slowly, from a group of Marina's friends, a girl in all white walked to the middle of the tent. Her friends huddled around Marina in anticipation. The girl was 17. Her white silk dress was heavily embroidered with tapering sleeves and leggings. Her thick black hair woven into a long strand down to her waist. The dress at the waist was tight, highlighting her bust. The dress was heavily pleated around her waist, drooping down till her knees. Her white feet were bare but for silver ankle bracelets with bells. She stopped and with her feet touching, she began to lift and press her feet giving the audience a whisper of her anklets. The crowd stopped and listened. As the music soared, she slowly raised her arms up into the sky, then bringing them to shoulder height, folded them over her breasts. The music roared and the girl twirled. The movement raised her dress into a small circle. She twirled again but faster. Then, in perfect concert with the beat, she stepped forward, backward, sideways, always arranging her hands in different motions. Her eyes coordinated with each pose of her delicate fingers. The bright lights shinning on her beautiful young face. She danced and the audience watched. The music soared and she moved faster and faster. She would suddenly stop and stand still, her long hair continuing to swing, wrapping itself around her body. The girls shouted and screamed with excitement. They knew the meaning of this dance.

Mona watched from inside the house through the window. The girl was introducing herself as marriageable. Since it was her friend's engagement, the occasion permitted it. The timing was also right. Had she been two years older, it would appear an act of desperation. A couple of years younger and she would be taken as loose and without shame. She was playing her cards right. And she knew it.

Mona looked at the group of old ladies intently evaluating the performance, measuring the girl's beauty and tasking their memories to instantly select the right boy that they would decide she should marry. Mona shrugged. How powerful it is to decide the life partner of another person. How much satisfaction these oldies must get out of seeing an arranged marriage take place. Their will. Their decision. Their mutual agreements fulfilled at the cost of yet another young couple. She looked at Aunt Pukhraj, thinking "That dreadful old woman. Every affair is her affair. Every issue is her issue." Mona counted the eleven couples that Aunt Pukhraj had led to the slaughter over the last twenty years. Now eyeing this poor lamb. Not that Pukhraj was alone. Her band of faithfuls toed her line, falling to her persuasiveness, her deceit and her total distrust of knowledge and education. If only she had an open mind. Only last year, she tied that worthless high school dropout with a young man who topped the central service exam. What a crime. And on the premise that they were cousins! Everybody around here is a cousin. Ah, but family does come first. The individual sacrifices for society. That's how it should be. If not her cousin, who would have wed that wretched soul? But it must be done with some sense of justice. Not Pukhraj style.

Mona was distracted from her thoughts by the antics of a little boy. He wore a light grey cotton shirt and matching shorts with green mountain shoes. She estimated he might be three years old. He walked among the other children but without any interaction with them. As if they did not exist. He paused, looked half way up and raised his fist. Mona tried to see who he was posing for but there was no one. He stood there for a few moments then returned to his aimless wandering around. She could see he was talking but realized there was no one he was addressing. Mona left the room for the courtyard and stood right in front of the boy. She called out but he did not register her presence. She held him gently by his shoulders but he made no eye contact.

He said "Ado no nah, ado no nah." Mona asked him his name. He kept looking somewhere else and repeated "Ado no nah, ado no nah." He then lowered his head and rolled his eyes up raising his hand over his head as if ready to fly. Mona stood behind him, placed her arms under his arms, locked her hands and twirled in a circular motion raising his feet off the ground. The boy smiled and laughed. He liked it. She continued for several circles until she felt dizzy and stopped. The boy walked away as if in search of something. His mother approached Mona and introduced herself, saying she was very worried about her son. He did not play with other kids. His vocabulary was decreasing and he wouldn't sleep. Mona told her how a friend had a similar child who improved drastically after his tonsils and adenoids were removed.

Sherdil saw Colonel Javed approaching with a big smile, rather pleased with himself having just seen off the General.

"Uncle, Uncle Sheru," Javed cried, warmly embracing his uncle. "Where have you been all evening? I was looking for you."

"Oh, I saw you were busy with your town friends so I tended to the servants. They don't seem to get anything right on their own," replied Sherdil.

"You should have joined us, we were discussing..."

"Politics followed by religion. Could there be another topic?" Sherdil asked.

"Yes, you are right. So, how's the food?"

Uncle glanced at the array of dishes full of roasted chicken, meatball sauce, basmati rice and the freshly baked bread. It looked and smelled delicious.

"It's great. Tell me, which hotel is catering?"

Javed laughed. "Uncle, this food comes from the military hospital."

"Are you feeding us hospital food?"

"No, no, no. Does this food look like it is meant for patients? It is specially prepared. You see, senior officers are entitled to such parties. The army kitchen is excellent and the cook is fantastic. But can't you see from how organized the arrangements are? Could a civilian caterer be so organized?"

Uncle had noticed that the servers were busy with some of the guests, noticeable by their short army haircuts, and that the rest were rather neglected.

"Tell, me, nephew, this must cost a lot."

"Well, actually it is subsidized by the army."

"I know. What I mean is that these feasts must cost the army a lot. I heard on the bus that a listing of army expenses was leaked."

"Uhu…" Colonel Javed was distracted by another guest.

***

"Sounds familiar, which movie is that?" Mona called out from the other room.

Before Marina could say anything, Sabina, who was visiting, leaned over the bed so that she could see into the other room and said "It is an old one, Aunti; Laila recommended it. *Pretty Woman*."

"You call that old. Well I guess so. I saw it in the cinema," Mona said, entering the room.

"They screened this in the cinema?" an astonished Sabina asked, taking the bowl of vermicelli from Mona.

"No, you dummy, Mama saw it when she was in the UK. Nobody would screen a movie like this here in our country. The Mullahs would hang them," Marina explained, helping herself to the sweets.

"Well, I saw *The Graduate* in a cinema here in Pakistan." Mona stood near the television. "It was a love story where a young man had an affair with a middle aged woman and then fell in love with her teenage daughter. In fact I saw it in Peshawar."

"In Peshawar?" Now Marina was astonished. "That place needs another five hundred years to become part of the 21st century."

The phone rang and before Sabina could turn her head towards the door, Marina had already raced into the next room to receive it. Sabina smiled to Mona, "It is him."

Moments later an angry Marina returned. "Mama, why do they have to use this number? Tell Papa to give his stupid office people the other number."

Sabina dropped her head onto the pillow. "Marina, the engagement was two weeks ago. He has been calling every day. He loves you."

"Does he, Mama?" Marina asked, curling her feet. She wrapped her arms around her legs.

"Of course," Mona replied, still looking at the movie.

"Mama, how can he love me; he hardly knows me." Marina was upset. "This isn't love, it's… it's… arranged."

Mona looked at her daughter. "Marina, we have discussed this."

"Mama, it is my life," Marina protested.

Mona removed the shawl from the bed and sat down beside her daughter. Sabina cuddled up anticipating something serious.

"Do you remember the pink dress I bought for your seventh birthday?"

"Yes, it was my favourite for many years. It still is."

"Do you remember how you cried refusing to wear it? At first, you didn't like it a bit."

"Yes, yes, but I had never worn it and didn't know how, how much I would fall in love with it."

"The difference between a love marriage and an arranged marriage is in who chooses."

"But I want to choose."

"No, you don't. What you want is a marriage that will last you a lifetime and bring you happiness and joy. When I, your Aunt, and Grandma chose this boy, it was because we thought he would provide that life to you. And yes, that he would love you."

"But Mama, loving a dress is not loving a person," Marina moaned.

"Everybody in the West has love marriages," Sabina offered with a sigh.

"And what do you know of love in the West? Enlighten us. You haven't even been as far as Karachi," Mona interjected.

Mona straightened herself up. Looking at the shawl, she gently rubbed the crease with her hand. With a slight movement of her head she began. "Every marriage is an attempt to secure happiness. In the West, the burden to choose a life partner is on the individual, with little support from others. The responsibility of such an important decision is not shared. They call it space, privacy, freedom." She turned her head towards the girls. "But others are necessary. They have experience, knowledge. If it weren't for Shahista's cousin's friend, we would not even have known of Adil."

"But in the West, girls can roam free. They can go anywhere. Anywhere. They can meet boys." Sabina was looking somewhere between the ceiling and the window.

"And what do you want to do when you meet boys?" asked Mona.

The girls blushed.

"In the West, if you don't meet the right boy during school, then your search is restricted to the office. Neighbours hardly meet. How many eligible bachelors roam around in any given office? And how many are of your liking? And how many of them would like you? And time is passing. Checkmate. Would you like to spend the best years of youth with the constant tension of finding a mate? The arranged marriage is a vetting process. A whole network of women has been on the lookout for you girls ever since you were born."

"Since we were born!" the girls echoed.

"Since you were born! Aunti Fareeda sent Chanbacha to his brother's house the day Seemi was born. What do you think they fought over?"

"But Aunti, they didn't know her. What if Seemi grew up to be a mass murderer?" asked Sabina.

"Sabina, the judgment on how Seemi would be raised was based on Fareeda knowing her sister and the house she ran. Based on knowing the family intimately and knowing how a young girl would be raised in our society, it was sound judgment. An investment. Not a blind shot. And you all see how Seemi has turned out."

"Yes Mama, but they can go wrong too."

"Yes my dear. There are no guarantees in marriage. Marriage is a gamble. You can win it all and you can lose. Nobody can predict with certainty how a marriage will turn out. But, all the more reason that many, and not just the two people, should be part of the decision making."

"But Mama." Marina was not satisfied.

"Would you rather meet boys and have to impress them with your dress, or lack of it, and be victim to their insults and rejections. Or would you rather serve tea to Adil's parents, in your own home, and let them evaluate you discreetly without insult. With your parents at hand to protect you. My dear, cherish life and love will come. Don't worry."

"Do you love Uncle Javed, Aunti?" Sabina blurted, half in jest and half serious.

Mona looked straight into Sabina's eyes then smiled. "It is time we got you settled too. You are getting out of hand, young lady. Tell your mother I shall be visiting her tonight."

CHAPTER 2

The Shrine was on the outskirts of the city at the foot of the beautiful Margalla Hills. As their car turned from the last row of houses, the road became bumpy. The grass along the road was tall, uncut. As the car drove past them, the water buffalo would turn their heads sleepily, showing little interest in anything but grass. The air smelled of a mix of wet grass and dung. The road weaved along an uneven surface. Mona kept changing gears to climb, descend, then again climb the rises. It was as if this part of the road was made when the engineers had gone home.

Marina was excited. This was her first visit to a shrine. As they approached the site, crowds began to appear. Men, women, cars and buffalo all occupied the road with a communist's sense of equality. Adding to the confusion were the rain and the numerous children. It was as if the young ones had sprouted out of the ground in response to the heavy rain earlier that morning. Marina could see the long bamboo poles with black, green and white flags. The smell had now changed to freshly cooked rice with saffron and cinnamon. She could see the amazingly colourful shops which were actually makeshift structures turned permanent. Worry beads, prayer mats, calendars with pictures of holy places were all exhibited for sale.

Mona turned the car to a spot in front of the shops and parked. She looked at Marina for a second then got out of the car, waving the crowding children away. They both climbed the steps into the courtyard. They removed their shoes at the landing and proceeded towards the main tomb. The white marble floor was cold to their bare feet. Marina adjusted her long shawl, draping her whole body, and made sure her head was completely covered. She noticed a group of women praying at the far end away from the tomb. There was a small group of men sitting beside the tomb chanting in heavy voices. They wore green dresses with heavy turbans and long beards. Most seemed undernourished. Mona approached the box beside the tomb and dropped some money in it. Marina raised her hands and was beginning to pray when a loud voice interrupted her. She looked to her side and saw a man waving ungraciously. "Women to that end, not here." Marina could not believe he meant her but he waved again, this time with a bigger frown. Mona had returned and pulled Marina away towards the other end of the tomb. "What was he saying?" Marina asked as they walked back towards the steps.

"I told you this was not a good idea." Mona said.

Placing her hand on Mona's shoulder for support, Marina slipped on her shoes. "Why was he so rude?" she asked.

"You were standing at the head-side of the grave. He told you to stand at the other end. Hadn't you noticed where the other women were?"

Marina was still puzzled. "What was he saying?"

"Women cannot stand at the head-side."

"But why?" asked Marina.

"Because they are unclean. That is what he was saying."

Marina blushed first with embarrassment then with anger and vowed never to visit a shrine again.

CHAPTER 3

The digital clock in the dashboard of his Honda Civic showed seven fifty-three. Kamran could see the tall Saudi-Pak Tower right ahead. He passed the large white marble sign "UN House" and the four flags fluttering in the winter breeze. The sun shone on the 19-story building to his right and he estimated that his car would be under the tower's shade for most of the day. He loved his car and didn't want its beautiful Sherwood green to fade under the intense sunlight.

He walked up the marble steps into the atrium. Passing the metal detector, he opened his briefcase for the male guard who greeted him with a nod and "OK." The guard did not use his hand-held metal detector to search Kamran. Kamran made his way through the narrow arches into the lift. The walls had mirrors and Kamran, standing six feet, could see himself over the crowd. He adjusted his tie. A cup of hot green tea was on his desk. The computer clock showed 7:58. He smiled. It always gave him pleasure to reach the office before time. He checked his calendar, went through his email and then prepared for the 9:00 meeting.

The meeting room was on the 9th floor. The United Nations Resident Representative entered the room at 9:03, apologizing for his delay. Other members were already seated with their tea and coffee. The room was small and the walls were mounted with large posters of the various UN organisations. The UNICEF poster showed poor African children in a school. The WFP poster was a plane dropping food packages. There were posters for the fight against drugs, the convention on human rights, and agricultural development. There were five women and seven men. They were of varying nationalities: African, European, Asian. All the men wore ties and jackets.

Two of the women wore *shalwar-kameez* and the other three wore western business suits.

The main item on the agenda was poverty alleviation. The Resident Representative spoke of how the year-old military government sought the UN's assistance in formulating a poverty reduction program for the country where 40% of the 130 million-strong population had an income of less than a dollar a day. Kamran, though listening, kept his eyes on some papers in front of him, occasionally editing a word here and there. Kamran's thoughts drifted to how for two weeks he had searched in vain for a squash court where he could play his favourite game. The only one for public use had a cement floor chipped in several places. The whitewash of the walls was peeling and the lights wouldn't work. He eventually found an excellent court. It had wooden floors, enamel paint and air-conditioning for summer. But it was an army court and civilians were not allowed.

The Resident Representative spoke of how keen the Planning Commissioner was on the poverty issue and how the government considered this a top priority. He allowed every member to speak. Given his turn, Kamran placed his pen down and with eyes focused on his papers locked his fingers together, lowering his back so that he almost touched the table with his chin.

"There are three issues here," he began, raising himself slightly. "First, the Planning Commission has no decision-making powers. Therefore, we should engage in a dialogue with the people who really do decide policy of the country. And that means the military. Titles in this country are misleading. Even during a civilian government, neither the Prime Minister nor the Parliament can alter the budget. They have no real powers. Second, over its fifty-year life, this country has had only one policy and that is to invest in the military at the cost of social development. That has been the policy during each and every government including the current one. Third, poverty reduction requires a fundamental shift in policy. A realignment of money from defence to health and education."

The UNICEF representative gave a big nod, and Kamran continued. "Large amounts of money. So far, nobody in the government has indicated such a shift in allocations. Therefore, this current drive towards poverty reduction is another charade."

Kamran took a breath and before anyone could speak, he continued. "Pakistan is not a poor country. The government has large amounts of money it chooses not to spend on its people. The people are poor because of the government's priorities. This is a crisis of priorities. Nothing else."

Without a word, the Chairman indicated the next person to speak. The lady to Kamran's left spoke with a British accent. "Securing peace is the best road to poverty reduction. And that means a resolution of the Kashmir issue."

The man from the Drug Control Agency spoke with a soft thin voice. "Yes, but that proposal is rather ethereal, don't you think?"

"Yes, I agree," interrupted the representative of the Food and Agriculture Organisation. "It is preaching."

The Chairman intervened before the lady could counter-argue. "Yes, we are not in the preaching business."

"Advocacy, yes, but preaching no," said Kamran with a smile. Everybody laughed. Turning his smile into a pout, the Chairman looked straight at Kamran. With elbows on the table and hands open he said, "I concede on all three points." He leaned back, took the bottom of his tie and tugged it straight over his shirt buttons. Though broad, the tie was a miserably feeble attempt to hide his enormous belly. Placing his arms on the armrest, he said, "But we must work within the confines given us." Kamran took a deep breath through his nose and nodded with disappointment.

Back at his office, Kamran called the motor pool to arrange for a car to take him to the Gender Sensitisation Workshop at the International Labour Organization office situated in the Diplomatic Enclave, Sector 5 of Islamabad. A young trainee at the UN central library had joined him in the vehicle. Construction along the route caused a detour and the car passed by the Canadian High Commission. There were large queues leading to the two small wickets outside the embassy. The trainee asked, "Kamran Sahib, how does one emigrate to Canada?"

"You get a form, fill it out, and submit it. There is a point system. If you qualify for 70 points, your application is accepted."

"On what basis is the application accepted?" asked the trainee.

"The criteria are provided in the booklet accompanying the form. They are clearly stated," Kamran replied.

"But, what are the real criteria? The hidden criteria?"

"I told you. It is all written in the book." After a pause, Kamran added, "You can't believe a government can be upfront and transparent?"

"No, of course not."

Kamran smiled. "There are some countries in the world where the people can trust their governments to a fair degree." They had arrived at the venue.

The facilitator finished her introduction by complaining that in Pakistan, property is exclusively owned by men and almost never by women. She emphasized that advocacy could improve the lot of women in society. Kamran intervened. "You speak as if the problem of treating women differently will go away with talks and explanations. But you miss the fundamental. There is a reason for every societal norm. To change behaviour, you must address the reason. Property is owned by men because ownership is established by shedding blood. Society, both men and women, have agreed that where there is killing, it should be amongst men, sparing women and children. That is the norm. In places where a property can be settled through courts and the police, ownership is not male exclusive. Did you know that most houses in Islamabad are registered to women? It is because in Islamabad you do not need a gun battle to settle ownership. As substitute institutions arise, so the norms adopt. People intrinsically believe in fair play. The apparent partiality of a system is in response to a constraint and not a result of bias against a particular group."

Most present did not agree with Kamran. But that didn't seem to matter to him. In fact, he was getting used to disagreement. What mattered most to him was that he spoke his mind without hesitation.

By the end of the day, Kamran was feeling tired. He checked his electronic scheduler and realized that a talk on the role of women in Islam was scheduled that evening at the Centre for Strategic Studies. The speaker was a renowned Islamic scholar from Japan. Kamran arrived a bit late and the lecture had already begun. The speaker praised the role Islam gave to women and pointed out how in the 7th century, barbaric Arab laws of inequality were replaced by enlightened principles of Islam. While listening to her speech, Kamran thought of the time, a few years ago, when he managed a computer centre for a government department. The cashier had brought a tall, thin bearded man to Kamran and introduced him as a member of the missionary Tablighi group. He was visiting from Algeria. As they sipped tea, in a calm, soft voice the man began preaching the tenants of Islam to Kamran. Kamran wondered for many years why, of the 300 staff at the department, the missionaries chose him for their onslaught. He felt offended then, and now, that someone should consider him less religious. Why, because he wore western clothes? Or because, unlike the rest, he knew how to use a computer? Perhaps because he was offering computer lessons instead of propagating religion.

    The guest speaker described how Islam treated women with respect and equality. She mentioned several women of the Sufi order. Kamran could not resist. During the discussion period, he asked her, "Is it Islam which is practiced in Islamic countries today? The reality is that women are subjected to massive inequalities contrary to the principles of Islam. What is practiced is not Islamic.

"I will explain through an example. Last year, while in England, my sister was asked by a local how she liked England. Her reply was, 'I like it. I can walk.' The inquirer pursued, 'What do you mean you can walk? Can't you walk in Pakistan?' My sister said, 'No, not without a chaperon. I cannot walk alone, not even at daytime.'"

"So you see, Madam speaker, the majority of Muslims today must adhere to a false interpretation of Islam. It is the hijacking of Islam. The irony is that our lives are dictated by this hijacked version and not the real Islam. Anybody who speaks against this hijacking is accused of blasphemy."

The speaker responded by admitting how few people understood the real Islam and how interest groups manipulated religion for self-interest. She concluded that unfortunately this was the case with every religion. She spoke of the need to read the Holy Book in a native language in addition to recitations in Arabic because most people did not speak or understand Arabic. The key to implementing a system is in understanding it.

CHAPTER 4

It was Sunday afternoon when Kamran drove from Islamabad to the twin city of Rawalpindi, or Pindi as locals preferred to call it. He had an appointment with a Colonel Javed who owned a house on the Peshawar road. Kamran wanted to buy a house in Islamabad but found the prices were too high. His agent gave him the number of the Colonel promising Kamran that he would like the house. Kamran passed by the Islamabad airport, which lay between the two cities, rather nearer to Pindi than Islamabad. The highway was decorated with coloured flags of no particular denomination. There were armed sentries posted every five hundred yards all the way from zero point (city centre) to the airport. Kamran thought it must be in preparation of a foreign dignitary's visit to Islamabad. Beyond the airport the road turned onto a bridge and then passed the old Presidency which had now been converted to a women's college. At the traffic lights he turned left noticing the two cannons at the gates of an army mess. This is general headquarters area, he told himself. He took another left passing by the Fauji Foundation offices and into the Lal Kurti bazaar, named for the Red Coats regiment stationed there during the British occupation.

There was a traffic jam. Mini buses blocked the road by stopping to drop and pick up passengers. Considering this to be a major bazaar, he wondered why there was no bus stand to accommodate the buses and their passengers. As he manoeuvred slowly past the buses, he noticed a large area of grass quite ideal for a bus stand. The area was barbwired and a goat was standing inside the enclave feeding on the grass. Behind the goat was a long wall with a large gate. Kamran pulled over and got out of the car. He approached the soldier guarding the gate and, pointing towards the traffic, said "It's a mess."

"Yes, sir, it is. It is the same every day. There are at least a couple of scuffles every day too. They really should build a bus stop."

"Where?"

"I don't know."

"How about there?" Kamran pointed to the goat.

"Oh no. Can't build one there."

"Why?"

"That's military land."

"So?"

"It would be a security threat."

Kamran read the sign on the gate, "Military Veterinary Hospital." He looked in through the open gates and could see a few horses.

"Security threat to horses," he thought, shaking his head and returning to his car. He turned by the sign that said "Officers Mess" and parked outside the

Colonel's house along the perimeter of the Army Boys School.

Colonel Javed was waiting for him. Kamran gave his car keys to the Colonel's driver who proceeded to park the car inside the gates to the massive house. Javed and Kamran jumped into the shinning Pajero truck. It had just been washed and the windscreen was still dripping with water. They drove past the same veterinary hospital and Kamran raised the issue of the traffic with Javed.

"These buses are a problem", said Javed.

"But buses are necessary to carry shoppers to and from the bazaar. Surely some arrangement should be made to resolve this perpetual traffic jam."

"Actually, all this area belongs to the military. We allow the civilians here but it really is military property." They passed the Fauji Foundation office and turned left. "I used to work at the

Foundation. It takes care of retired army personnel. It also runs several industries including cement and corn flakes."

They passed the military museum and could see the tanks and armored vehicles on display. Javed pointed to a sign on the left. "Have you been to the CSD? It's a market for army personnel. You can buy anything from soap to motorcycles at subsidized rates. They sell chickens, handicrafts. The gas station there is run by the military so the fuel is good quality."

Kamran nodded. "I have seen the place. They even have their own barber."

They turned right and passed the military hockey stadium, the military cricket grounds and the army Askari Bank. "Tell me, Colonel. The army has its own schools?"

"Yes. You see, officers get posted all over the country. Without schools to accommodate them their children's education would suffer."

"The army has its own hospitals?"

"Yes, where would you bring your wounded during war? The civilian hospitals barely function."

"The army has its own shopping centres, residential areas, recreation centres."

"Yes."

"They have their own bank and credit cards."

"Yes."

"Is it true that a civilian government or even Parliament could not touch the defence budget allocations?"

"They would invite a coup if they tried," said Javed.

"Then how else would you define a state within a state? Or an occupation army?"

"But the army defends the country. Surely their expenses must be met. Nobody wants to spend on defence unless it is necessary."

"I guess you are right. I just wonder, if they are not willing to give a piece of waste land for a much-needed bus stand, whose interest are they serving anyway?"

"Young man, defence is the first priority. Have you seen combat?"

"No. Of course not."

"No wonder. These bookish ideas would flee you once you tasted the horrors of war." They passed a large military hospital and the military polo grounds before they stopped. Kamran did not like the house and excused himself by saying it was not inviting.

CHAPTER 5

The American centre was located on Jinnah Avenue a couple of kilometres east of the Saudi-Pak Tower. It was another hectic Monday at the UN offices, and Kamran had just finished saving a PowerPoint presentation on his computer. He looked at the computer clock, which indicated 4:45. He knew he could get to the American Centre in five minutes but wanted to get there earlier to secure a good seat. He liked to hear Dr. Tahir Banuri speak. Tahir was one of very few people who impressed Kamran. Everything Tahir said made sense. Even where he disagreed, Kamran appreciated the structured approach Tahir took in presenting his viewpoint. Tahir researched his topic well and kept remarkably up to date. What Kamran liked most was how seamlessly Tahir could shift from economics to environment to sociology to development. He was an academic, scientist, and policymaker all in one. He would interject quotes from a broad spectrum of thinkers and books. He was not a single subject specialist who could only debate with a narrow background but understood the view of multiple and competing disciplines. Kamran did not know the other two speakers, a retired army general and a journalist. The topic was dimensions of human security.

He reached for his glove compartment and fished out a pirated CD he had bought from the Pindi bazaar. As he stopped at the traffic lights, a small boy in tattered clothes approached his car. He couldn't be more than nine years old. His hands and face were dirty as if he hadn't had a bath since winter began. The sleeveless sweater he wore was too small for him, leaving his stomach half bare. He was shivering with cold. He put his hand out and asked for money. Kamran lowered the window and felt the cold wind. He looked around and saw two other kids begging from other cars. On the other side of the road, he could see a woman beggar carrying a baby. That must be the mother, he thought. For a moment he considered whether paying the child would encourage begging. Then he pulled out a fifty rupee note and gave it to the child. As the light turned green, Kamran drove ahead thinking about the child. He turned the music off. It did not feel right.

Kamran parked his car near the massive satellite dish antenna outside the American Centre. He walked past the concrete barriers which were erected after a mob had burnt the centre down a decade ago. He entered the narrow door, went through the metal detector, passed the armed security guard, and entered the main hall. The platform was decorated with a white sheet and flowers. Three speakers and a convener were seated. Dr. Banuri was in his late forties but looked older due to his grey hair, beard and horn-rimmed glasses. The general was short and bald and sat in the middle. The journalist wore a cap, casually dressed as if he had just returned from a game of golf.

The journalist mainly focused his discussion on the country's rice and cotton crops and how the markets would respond if production were to be increased. He used a lot of financial terms and did not try to simplify for the non-technical audience. The General was adamant that without a strong defence, a country could not even consider economic growth or social development.

Dr. Banuri started with the acknowledgment that a nation must be able to defend itself but then questioned the validity of some common assumptions. First, it was assumed that the only form of defence is military. He cited the USSR as being a military superpower that nonetheless broke up because of social unrest. A second assumption was that the money currently spent on the military was actually contributing to the defence of the nation. One-third of the nation's annual budget was allocated to defence, but a large portion of this money was spent on pensions. A soldier retires at the age of thirty-five after 18 years of service. He then receives a pension for the rest of his life. He and his dependents receive medical benefits for the rest of their lives. Every year more and more servicemen retire and add to the burden on the pension fund. This was an exponential growth that needed an increase in budget every year. He asserted, the army was weary of institutions that may curtail its power and has stifled the judiciary, education, even democracy. The cost of this was phenomenal. Even to sustain the army, economic growth was necessary. And the route to growth was investment in social development through health and education.

The general agreed that the situation of poverty and unemployment was grave.

Then, as an afterthought, he said the population was growing and that was the main problem. If it weren't for this massive population growth, things would not have been so bad.

Kamran could not resist and put a question to the General: "You speak of population as a problem. How can people be the problem? The State exists for people, not the other way around. It is lack of investment in health and education which results in population growth."

"I agree, we must increase investments in health and education," the general interjected.

"We all understand that part. But where to get the money for this investment? Which part of our expenses do we cut?"

"It is a chicken or egg problem," said the General.

"But aren't you assuming that the money currently allocated to defence is actually spent on defence? What about wastage, or spending on non-essentials, or corruption?"

"Such as?"

"Like the army squash courts in Peshawar. They were built at a time when the chief of army staff had refused orders from the Prime Minister to relocate the ammunitions depot away from settled areas. The reason he cited was that they did not have funds to carry out the relocation."

The general was firm. "Defence must be a first priority. First, you must secure a nation in which you can create an atmosphere of development. Without a nation, you have nothing."

CHAPTER 6

The evening sun was setting. Sabina and Marina were strolling on the roof terrace. Each had her arms locked around her stomach. Traffic, mostly mini-busses and motorcycles, passed below. The mini-busses were full with men hanging at the rear. As they passed, the men would look up at the house and the girls. The girls were aware of this but ignored the glares.

"What should I tell my friend? She is confused and scared. One day there was nothing. The next day there is a man, a family and a wedding date." Sabina said.

After a moment's thought, Marina replied confidently, "She should perform an *Istikhara*. It is a prayer for guidance. You have to take a bath at night. Then pray and request God for guidance. There are certain holy verses you recite at bedtime. Then you sleep. God will guide you through your dreams."

"What if you don't dream anything?"

"Then that is God's reply. Dreams have meaning. But tell her, if she performs an *Istikhara*, whatever the dream, she must fulfil it. If the dream tells her this boy is good for her, she must marry him."

"Or what?"

"She will face the wrath of God. You must do as the dream dictates. But dreams need an interpreter. Not everybody can interpret the true meaning of a dream."

The sun could not be seen anymore. Clouds on the horizon were bright pink with the setting sun's light. They heard a couple of knocks on a nearby loudspeaker, then a blow, a couple of coughs and then the call for prayer: "Allah o Akbar, Allah o Akbar…" The girls draped their scarves over their heads. A few seconds into the first call, another loudspeaker erupted, then another and another. Soon a dozen speakers were reciting the call for prayer. The sound which at first was clear and soothing now became a blare, and as the earlier speakers finished, the words became more distinguishable: "Come to prayer, come to righteousness, there is no God but Allah."

"Every item in a dream has a meaning. For example," Marina continued, "blood means money. Water means happiness. White is good. A flower means a son."

"What's a flower got to do with a son?" Sabina asked.

"A flower means a son," Marina spoke forcefully. "Last year my grandmother dreamt that her late husband gave her two roses. Within two months, she was blessed with two grandsons."

Sabina let loose her arms and took a deep breath "I don't think she should marry if she doesn't like him. You can't decide your future life on a dream."

"It is not just a dream. It is divine guidance. Ask your mother. I'm sure her marriage was decided through *Istikhara*."

"Are you saying every marriage is based on a dream?"

"Almost every one. Of course they would not perform an *Istikhara* if other factors do not support the decision. *Istikhara* is performed when a very important decision is to be made and you are undecided."

Below on the road, a thin man was cycling with half a dozen clothes on hangers draped over his shoulder. There were freshly ironed army uniforms and men's and women's *shalwar-kameez*.

Sabina confessed, "All I know is that the night I do not brush my teeth, I have a bad dream. Or the night I eat something that causes gas."

"Sabina, don't make fun of religion."

"I don't believe all marriages are decided on dreams."

"Well then, let us ask your mother."

They went downstairs through the living room into the bedroom at the back of the house. Mona was prostrating on the prayer mat. Her scarf draped her head and upper body. She raised her head and sat back on her legs, turned her head first right then left before fixing her gaze at the point she had touched with her forehead. She raised her slim hands together, palms facing upwards. Her lips were moving and her lovely face showed reverence. A slight frown and concerned eyes with rapidly blinking long eyelashes made her look uniquely vulnerable and yet at the same time satisfied.

She completed her prayer by running her palms over her face. She turned her head and with one hand folded the top corner of the prayer mat. She had needed only a second to come out of the experience and was now standing looking at the girls.

Marina approached the prayer mat and began her prayers. She performed the same motions and had the same frown. But it was not the same.

Mona pointed Sabina to another mat that was lying folded on the sewing machine. Sabina picked it up, laid it out beside Marina and began to pray. Khadija, Sabina's heavy-set middle-aged mother, returned from the adjacent bedroom carrying worry beads in her right hand. She removed the scarf from her head and draped it across her chest and shoulders. She sat on the bed and folded her legs. "Age is getting to me. Once I sit down, my knees won't let me rise again," she complained to Mona.

Mona sat besides Khadija on the bed. Gently touching her arm, Mona said, "It is not your age that keeps you seated, Khadija. It is your weight." Raising scarves to cover their mouths, both laughed.

The girls had finished their prayers. First Sabina, then Marina.

Marina spoke to Khadija: "Aunti, tell Sabina about *Istekhara*." Sabina sat behind

Mona on the bed. Marina pulled up a small footstool and sat on it.

"Children, these are grave matters."

"Was your marriage decided upon an *Istikhara*?"

"Almost every marriage is."

"See!" Marina glanced at Sabina.

"And yours, Mona Aunti?" asked Sabina.

Mona briefly smiled; then, looking down at the bedcover and slowly passing her hand over it, "No. Our marriage was decided by my parents. Javed's parents proposed and my parents accepted."

"Just like that?"

"It was the decent thing to do. When a decent, respectable family with a son proposes to a self-respecting family with a daughter of age, what is there to resist?"

"But there was no love," Marina interjected.

"There always is love," Khadija intervened. "The love of a teenager is not the only love. Love has many forms. There is love for God. Love for children. Love for your house. My garden. Love for cats and billy goats. Love for food, which I must prepare before Sabina's father arrives." Khadija began to slowly rock, picked herself up and waddled out of the room. "Thanks for tea, Mona; God bless you," she said with a wave of her hand.

"Aunti, are dreams true?" Sabina asked.

"Yes. But not all of them. You should not be frightened of dreams. And you should not believe in every dream you have."

"But Mama, it is part of our faith," Marina said.

"That is where we women go wrong. I know of one who nearly broke her marriage because she dreamt her husband was with another woman. Of course, later in life she found out it was not true. She had a lovely husband and lovely children. She almost lost all. There was nothing divine about her dream. It was just her insecurity manifesting itself in her subconscious."

"But then how do you recognize the divine ones?"

"You can't."

Sabina saw victory in this and rising up she said, "I'm going to have some tea."

CHAPTER 7

Javed was still grooming himself in the bathroom. Mona and Marina were waiting in the car. The trip to their village would take three hours, and they wanted to start early to avoid the midday heat. Finally, Javed emerged wearing a light beige *shalwar-kameez* and a short sleeveless coat. He wore a red silk handkerchief in the coat pocket. His heavy cologne spread wherever he went. Javed gave some final instructions to the servant who held the gate open. They would be home shortly after sunset. Mona sat in the front passenger seat with her white chador draped over her head and shoulders. Marina spread out on the backseat. She left her chador folded on the seat.

Javed manoeuvred the car slowly through Lal Kurti bazaar. He stopped to buy two large boxes of *barfi*, the sweets that were the family's favourite. As the bazaar ended and military land began, the road widened into a highway. They passed the military hospitals and the army polo ground. Another twenty-minute drive west brought them out of the city. An hour later they passed through the historic city of Taxila.

Javed reminded Marina, "Taxila was the seat of the Gandhara civilization two thousand years ago."

"Were they Christians?" "No, this was pre-Christianity. It was a rich civilisation. One day we should visit the Taxila museum and see the artefacts from that era."

Marina was not interested in museums. She kept adjusting the sunscreen on the left window. Mona looked at the beautiful marble and onyx items displayed in shops alongside the road. There were tables, vases, tea sets, ashtrays, all in multiple colours of purple, orange, green, beige, white, grey and black. She asked Javed to stop. He turned off the road onto the dirt shoulder causing a large dust cloud. As the car stopped and the cloud thinned, a short stout man approached them. He had an onyx bowl in his hand. Presenting it to Mona, he said it was excellent for grinding cinnamon and cardamom. Mona nodded. She selected a beige table, two feet high with a round top. She asked for its price and immediately offered 30% less. He agreed. Javed mumbled about its getting late and said it was a waste of money.

They passed the cantonment city of Wah. A large sign prohibited unauthorised personnel from entering the cantonment area. An army check post was screening motorists wishing to enter the cantonment. The highway was wide and Javed could now speed, occasionally slowing down for the bullock carts travelling on the wrong side of the road and for children crossing the road with their herds of goats. He ignored the cyclists, hoping they would not turn while he sped by them. The road now meandered and they could see glimpses of the mighty Indus river. They passed an ancient tomb resting right in the middle of the highway. The roads swung around the dilapidated tomb. A few minutes ahead, the walls of the Attock fort ran along the road. As they approached the large bridge spanning the Indus river, a sign said, "Good bye, Government of Punjab." On the bridge, they could see the Attock fort on the left bank of the river. Javed told Marina that the perimeter wall ran well under the water.

"It is rumoured that the Mughals built an underground tunnel to connect the two provinces. This was the western-most citadel of the Mughal armies. Akbar the Great had constructed this fort."

"What is it used for now?" asked Marina.

"Now it is used as a jail for political prisoners," Mona interjected.

Halfway across the bridge, they could see two mighty tributaries merging on their right. This is where Kabul River from Afghanistan and Swat River from Kashmir merge.

Marina could see the Kabul River water was muddy brown. The Swat River was clear, glacier water.

"The river is high due to the monsoon rains. It will remain high till September. The Swat River source is the Himalayas. The Kabul River's source is the Hindu Kush mountain range. Do you know that there is a point on the Pakistan-Afghanistan border where the three highest mountain ranges of the world meet? The Wakhan valley."

"Which is the third range?"

"The Karakoram. K2 is the highest peak in Karakoram and the second highest in the world."

"Which country is K2 in?"

"Pakistan. Don't they teach you anything at school?" Javed asked.

"Your father sometimes dilutes facts of geography with patriotism," said Mona.

"If there is no patriotism, there is nothing," offered Javed, rather pleased with his display of general knowledge.

They crossed the bridge and stopped at the toll station. The roadside sign said "Welcome to NWFP." Marina draped her chador over her head. Mona opened the ashtray under the cassette player and picked up a ten Rupee note. She handed it to Javed, who had rolled down his window to pay the clerk.

"You don't have to pay toll, Papa. You are military and are therefore exempt."

'I know, dear. I could claim that and avoid payment. He wouldn't dare ask for identification."

"It is only a small sum," Mona said. "Pay it. Also, you *were* military. You are now a retiree." "Mona, once military, always military. If there were a war, I could be called for duty. That's why I maintain my rank and should also be entitled to all benefits. The military are not like civilians. Once you retire, you are nobody. The military takes care of its own." Handing the money to the clerk, he placed the car in gear and drove on, not bothering to collect the receipt.

"You are entitled to medical facilities even during retirement, aren't you, Papa?"

"Oh, yes. My parents, wife and children are too."

"No, they aren't. They are covered only while you are in service," Mona protested.

"Well, strictly speaking you are right. But practically, we always get away with it. You see, child, loyalty is a great virtue. Not everybody has it. It comes with training and discipline. Look at the politicians, arrested in the coup, lying in that fort. They were betrayed by their own civilian subordinates."

"They were betrayed by the military, Javed," Mona politely pointed out.

"The military has to interfere and remove corrupt politicians. It is in national interest. You can't just let these nobodies plunder the national exchequer."

Another forty minutes of driving and they reached the busy bazaar of Jehangira. Javed stopped at the kebab house and ordered kebabs. The kebabi asked Javed if he wanted eggs. Javed nodded and told him it was for a special occasion, he was visiting his home village. A beggar approached. The kebabi reached behind and fetched a piece of bread, placed a couple of kebabs on the bread, rolled it up and gave it to the beggar, who mumbled something in appreciation and left. By now the kebabs were cooking and Javed was enjoying the aroma. The kebabs were placed in a piece of newspaper, then in a plastic bag. Three small bags of yogurt were added to the package. Javed paid, returned to the car and placed the kebabs in the trunk. The strong aroma filled the car and now both Mona and Marina were dying to get to their destination and have their meal.

Javed turned right, leaving the highway onto a smaller road. Here he had to drive slowly. It was a narrow road with two-way traffic. The shoulder was dirt, and every time he moved to the left to make way for oncoming traffic, a dust storm would rise. There was a large, shallow pit in the right half of the road. A motorcyclist approached from the opposite direction. The rider was wearing goggles. A child, Javed estimated to be four years old, sat in front of him. A younger child sat in front of this child on the petrol tank. Two older children sat behind the rider. The last one was sitting on the steel carrier. Nobody was wearing a helmet. Trying to avoid the pit, the biker moved into Javed's right of way. Simultaneously, Javed steered into the pit causing the car to bump several times before it passed the hurdle. Both Javed and the bike rider went through this lane-changing manoeuvre as if it were a daily routine. Having passed each other, both drivers moved back to their proper lanes.

"How long has this pit been here, Papa?" asked Marina.

"It was here when I first visited your father's village, just after our marriage," Mona explained.

"The plans for this road were prepared ten years ago. The government just has not had enough money to carry it out. Maybe next year," Javed added.

Fields of wheat, corn and sugar cane were on either side of the road. Small canals crisscrossed the fields. Footpaths of mud were built on the perimeter of the fields. There were smaller patches of home gardens with spinach, tomatoes and mustard. They entered the main village by crossing a wooden bridge over a narrow canal. The houses had high mud walls. Occasionally, they would pass a brick house belonging to a richer family. Children, goats and cows adorned the dirt roads. Chicken wandering out from houses along the road were abundant. Javed had to drive very slowly to avoid the human and animal traffic and also to lessen the dust being raised by the vehicle. Some boys started running after the car. A couple of them recognized Javed and ran ahead into a house with brick walls. Shortly after, Uncle Sherdil emerged.

A broad smile erupted on Javed's face as he saw his uncle. Parking the car along the wall, he emerged and with open arms embraced Sherdil, who hugged Javed tight then greeted Mona. He placed his hand on Marina's head and kissed her forehead. Javed gave the kebab package to a boy and asked him to carry it inside. He carried the boxes of sweets himself. Sherdil told the other boys to go and play.

The house was a large courtyard surrounded by rooms. There were two rooms and a kitchen to the east and two rooms and the bathroom on the south side. The rooms opened into an L-shaped veranda that lead to the courtyard. The rooms were scantly furnished, each having a bed and some light furniture. Ceiling fans were installed in each room. The veranda had two large pedestal fans and two *charpoys* cluttered with very large solid pillows for people to rest on. There were another two *charpoys* in the courtyard. Along the north wall of the courtyard, a servant woman sitting on a low wooden stool was washing dishes and placing them on a *charpoy* to dry in the sun. Javed bent slightly so that his mother, a grey-haired elderly woman who walked with difficulty, could kiss his head. The women of the house embraced Mona and Marina and shook hands with Javed. The embraces were long. Marina was kissed on her head and forehead repeatedly. All the women spoke simultaneously with no audience in particular. Petty questions on when did they leave Pindi, did they have any problem on the way, and why didn't they bring their cousin with them. Sherdil had to quiet them down, reminding them it was Friday and the guests would like to have their lunch before the midday prayer.

Marina was enjoying all the attention. There was a certain genuineness in their reception that she missed when visiting people in the city. Marina felt she did not have to pose or present herself. There was total acceptance. Everything was so simple. The children from the street had now gathered and sat on the floor in the courtyard watching the visitors. A few chickens had also returned and walked around the courtyard plucking at wheat and corn seed stuck between the loosely-meshed floor bricks. Marina's eye was caught by a particularly vocal rooster who kept running under the *charpoys*, into the kitchen and back into the courtyard.

"Look at this rooster. He seems very busy," Marina said.

"He is only four months old. But a noisy fellow. Do you like him? You could take him back to Pindi," her aunt replied.

"Oh no, Aunti, he just seems cute and comical." Pointing to the rooster, her aunt made a gesture to the woman who had just completed washing the dishes.

Sherdil pointed to the bathroom and told his guests to refresh themselves.

"What a great thing that German project did for us. They built a drainage and sewerage system for most of the village. We have flush system in almost every house. Yes, the old days were harsh. We had to go to outhouses in the fields in the cold. Dawn was the only discreet time."

Sherdil's wife said, "To be honest, I like the old system. Ultimate privacy. Toilets in a house: disgraceful. There is no privacy whatsoever. Everybody knows when you go, how long you take. They can even hear you."

"Gul Bibi, stop it!" Sherdil protested.

"Why, it's true. Uncle Dildada was 97 years old when the doctor advised him not to go outside and to use the indoor toilet. He refused till the end."

Sherdil now turned to Javed. "Actually, he refused till the last day. He was suffering from pneumonia. He left the house early morning one day in the chill of December. Although he managed to come back, he died later that day. But the man never compromised."

"Perhaps it is what killed him," Javed noted.

"Everyone must die one day. He kept his dignity. That's what matters,' Sherdil responded.

By now it was noon and the sun shone directly on the courtyard. They retired into a room. The room had no lights on and had a high ceiling. A TV sat on a small coffee table in the far corner. A two-seater sofa set was placed along the wall. At the other end of the room was a closet built into the wall. A bed lay under this closet so that the closet doors opened over the bed. The men sat on the sofa while the women sat on the carpet and the children huddled in front of the TV. The old lady slowly climbed on the bed. She lay halfway down supported by large pillows. The maidservant entered the room leaving her slippers outside and sat with the children watching TV.

There was a knock on the door. The servant was already up and going out when Javed's aunt asked her to see who it was. She opened the door slightly to peek, immediately placed her *chador* on her head and greeted Mullah Sahib, who coughed loudly a couple of times before entering the house. The other women draped their heads. Javed and Sherdil received Mullah Sahib and seated him on the sofa. "I had heard Javed was coming today and wanted to see him," said Mullah Sahib.

With the new millennium due in a few months, the TV was now showing a documentary celebrating man's achievements. Old clips of an astronaut taking his first step on the moon were screened. There were shots of astronauts walking and bouncing around on the surface of the moon. The conversations had stopped for a moment and everybody watched TV. The maidservant, after a moment's contemplation, said, "They just don't have anything better to do" and left for the kitchen.

After short, polite exchanges, Mullah Sahib left for the mosque. Javed went to the bathroom for ablutions and Sherdil sat on the courtyard stool used earlier for dish washing. He turned the tap on and washed his hands, face, forearms and feet. Neither man used a towel. They placed small white cotton caps on their heads and proceeded to the mosque.

On the way, Sherdil asked Javed, "What is this we keep hearing about a report listing huge military expenses?"

"There was a rumour that a list of major defence expenditures had been leaked. But there is no truth to it," replied Javed.

"A neighbour whose son works in Dubai says the report is available abroad. It shows the extravagant spending on senior army officers and the amounts of kickbacks involved in the tank deals of last year. It tells how army planes are used, free of charge, for family picnics and other activities."

"I don't think such a report exists. These extravagant rumours have been around since the army first took over government in the 1960s. Army expenses are one of the best-guarded secrets of this country. Leakages are not possible."

INTERNAL AFFAIRS   Asif Niazi

The sermon had already begun. The mosque was not very large and Mullah Sahib's use of a microphone was more for the loudspeaker that broadcast for the benefit, or inconvenience, of those not present. He was describing TV and radio as elements of Satan. "They fill minds with lies and ill thoughts. These instruments were created by the devil himself in America. They say they landed a man on the moon. A what? A man. On what? The moon. They say they landed a man on the moon. That is what they say. All praise to Allah. A man on the moon. And how did the man get to the moon? They say on a large plane. A very large plane. Now you tell me. How many of you have seen an airplane? And how may of you have seen the moon? We see it every night. You have seen a plane. You have seen the moon. I have seen a plane. I have seen the moon. All praise to Allah. Three hundred men can sit in one plane and it still would not be full. How many? Three hundred. And it still would not be what? Full. Yes. Three hundred. Now you tell me. Can you seat three hundred men on the moon? Can you? Have you seen the size of the moon? How can you land such a large plane on such a small moon? These are the lies infidels feed us through the immoral devices of TV and radio. Corrupting our youth and our women. Down with the liar and his devices. Praise be to Allah." As he rose for prayer, the congregation, including Javed and Sherdil, assembled behind him. Mullah Sahib led and everyone else followed.

As they left, the boy who had earlier carried the kebabs joined them. A beggar sitting outside the mosque called out to Faiz "Help this poor man for a prayer". Sherdil gave him some money. As they proceeded, the boy asked Sherdil "what was he saying?"

"He will pray for us," replied Sherdil.

Looking back at the beggar, noticing his miserable condition, the boy asked "Why doesn't he pray for himself?"

Javed chuckled "Indeed. Why doesn't he pray for himself?"

The men returned home and lunch was served in the same room where they had watched TV. A sheet was spread out on the carpet. Dishes of chicken, rice and the kebabs Javed brought, spinach, yogurt and large cakes of bread were lined in the middle of the sheet. Everybody sat around the sheet on the carpet. Marina reached for the kebab and yogurt. Her aunt placed a chicken leg in her plate. Marina praised the chicken even though she enjoyed the spicy kebabs more. *Lassi*, a cold, salted, yogurt drink was served. There was brown wheat bread and white corn bread. Mona took some spinach and yogurt. Using her fingers, she wrapped spinach and yogurt in a piece of corn bread and ate. The meal was followed by very sweet green Chinese tea.

By now the sun had receded from most of the courtyard. They returned to the *charpoys* in the veranda and had the sweets that Javed had brought from Pindi. Seeing the chicken, Marina asked her aunt where the rooster was hiding. "Honey, you just ate it."

The heavy food and *lassi* were taking their toll. The women were starting to doze off. The journey had tired Mona and she now lay back on a pillow. Javed and Sherdil left the house to pay condolences to a family member whose father had died three days ago. They walked through the narrow village gullies. Wastewater poured from houses into open drains along the lanes. Javed pulled his *shalwar* up to avoid getting dirty. Enroute, Sherdil knocked on a door and two young men came out of the house and joined them. The group finally reached a very large walled courtyard with massive ancient wooden doors. The main doors were closed and a small wicket door carved from within the main door was being used for traffic. Javed and Sherdil entered directly into a large courtyard with 20 *charpoys* scattered. A small room stood at the far end. Each *charpoy* had several people on it. Some were lying down, some were seated. Their cousin was sitting on a *charpoy* near the door, flanked by two men.

As they approached, everybody rose. Javed hugged his cousin and offered his condolence. He then proceeded to hug the other people there. Some he recognized, some he did not but he knew, according to tradition, there was a representative from each village household. It would be embarrassing to the family if nobody turned up for the mourning. Each of the visitors hugged each of the mourners. This process took some time. Once seated, everybody raised their hands and quietly recited religious verses for a minute. The bereaved cousin folded his hands followed by others and last by Javed. After a few polite enquires on how the deceased died, Javed requested leave. He raised his hands again and the prayer was repeated. Javed hugged his cousin and left. Once outside, he thought what a waste. So many able bodied people doing absolutely nothing for days. No wonder this place doesn't develop.

Back home, Javed brought the onyx table from the car and presented it as a gift to his hosts. Sherdil and his wife thanked Javed for it. "It is so beautiful. You shouldn't have." On the way back to Pindi, Javed asked Mona "It was for them, wasn't it?"

"Of course it was," Mona replied.

Marina was thinking of her trip to the village. "Mama, I like visiting these people. They leave you with a good feeling."

Mona answered "Yes, dear. They are simple people. You visited their home, gave them time, and that was enough for them to like you and take interest in your life. You don't need credentials to secure their warmth. Credentials such as money, education, intellect, beauty. You are Javed's daughter and that is enough for them to love you."

"Don't be fooled by these people you call simple," Javed added. "Their interpersonal relations have been practiced for centuries and are refined. Since we have moved to the city, we have had to adapt to city life in a few generations. Our interpersonal skills are not as refined as our village cousins. These villagers are well grounded. We urbanites are confused."

CHAPTER 8

Kamran had just packed his briefcase and was about to leave his office when the phone rang. It was his longtime friend Major Zahid.

"Just called to remind you of this evening's programme at the officer's mess in Rawalpindi."

"I am not so sure. A bunch of over-rated soldiers bragging about their cars and cellphones is nothing to look forward to," replied Kamran.

"You forgot the satellite dish antennas. The latest fad is to brag over the number of channels you can view on your antenna. Don't worry. It is a mixed gathering. We may get lucky."

"You mean you may get lucky."

"I'll pick you up at six."

"OK."

***

Zahid arrived half an hour late. They drove down the highway, past the airport and turned left into the 10th Corps army compound.

"I am trying a short cut to promotion," said Zahid. "If I succeed I can usher young captains to far-flung areas on assignment and seduce their wives."

"Do you guys still do such things?" Kamran asked.

"It has become difficult with all this religion business. The golden age is over. Another fallout of the Afghanistan war. I say, why the hell did the Afghans have to kick the Russians out anyway? All the Russians wanted to do was build roads, schools and hospitals. Not to mention the constant supply of good vodka. Nothing constructive has happened in that wretched country since the Russians left. Still, not all officers are mullahs. Some are pretty lively."

They passed a small mosque and at the roundabout turned right, passing the army sports complex. The evening sun was still bright. The road was wide with little traffic. Large colonial-style houses were on both sides of the road. A black Toyota with black tinted windows passed them. The sidewalk was narrow and high. Kamran saw a small group of ladies walking leisurely along the road. Their car passed a cyclist with one hand on the handle and the other holding hangers from which hung two khaki uniforms and four ladies' *shalwar-kameez*.

"Is that all you have these poor soldiers do for you, iron clothes?" mocked Kamran, pointing at the cyclist.

"Of course not. They cook food, transport the children and the all-important, wash our cars. They also fetch groceries, tend the lawns, change light bulbs, open and close gates, receive guests and mind the phone. If the royal family in

England can have butlers, we can have batmen."

"How about maintaining the house?"

"No, that is what the army maintenance department does. It is a bit too technical for a batman." Another black Toyota with tinted windows pulled out of a large house.

They had approached the end of the road. To the right, a brass sign said "Officers' Mess." They passed through a large gate and turned left into the parking lot. They walked towards the building and stepped onto the veranda. The building looked old but was well maintained. Along the walls were decorations of shields and group photographs of previous members. Kamran stopped to look at the photos. There were large framed pictures of late generals Ayub and Zia and the current general and president Musharraf.

Zahid said, "See how graceful our presidents look in uniform."

"I just see a bunch of soldiers guilty of high treason."

"Kamran, this is an army mess, not a university campus. Be careful what you say."

They had come to the end of the U-shaped building. In the centre stood two tall poles. On one flew a flag of the 10th Corps and the other had the national flag. A large oval lawn stretched in front of the building beyond the flag posts. The entire lawn was encircled by a flower bed of roses and jasmine. The edge of the lawn was lined by small, whitewashed bricks neatly laid at an angle one after the other.

Kamran and Zahid left the corridor, passed the flags and stepped onto the lawn. There were large, round wooden tables carefully placed with ample distance between them. Each table had a white starched tablecloth and four easy armchairs. On the two sides along the flowerbed were stands with dishes of food.

There were about 50 people gathered, mostly couples. Some sat on the chairs while most stood chatting and sipping cola from glasses. Neatly dressed waiters were roaming with trays of cold drinks and water. The waiters wore black pants, white shirts and large starched Indian turbans.

At the far end of the lawn were two large, leather sofa sets. No one sat on them. Kamran assumed these were for the senior officers. He noticed Colonel Javed in a group busy laughing. A woman in a dark blue dress stood by the Colonel. She was looking at the flags. Her dark *shalwar-kameez* contrasted with her fair complexion. Her long black hair let loose in the light breeze. The guest of honour, the wife of the commanding officer of 10th Corp, arrived. A simple awards ceremony took place. Names of recipients were read out and each approached to receive a plaque from the guest of honour. The men bowed to the general's wife, took their awards and returned to their tables. Immediately after the ceremony, food was served on stands with large dishes and small stoves lit under them. There was basmati rice, roasted chicken, kebabs and chicken tikka. The food was delicious and everybody praised it. Some people left immediately after the meal. Others sat at the tables where tea was served. Kamran and Zahid sat at a table along with a couple of officers. Javed, noticing Kamran, told his wife, "There is that fellow who saw our house the other day. He didn't like it. Said it was not inviting. Whatever that means." He wandered towards them. Mona followed. The men rose and Kamran greeted Javed, slightly bowing his head towards Mona. A waiter pulled up another table and brought two more chairs.

"So what do you make of our simple ceremony, Kamran Sahib?"

"Forgive me Colonel, but our army is a composition of ceremonies and little else. Building confidence through medals, trophies and ranks eases the fear felt by anyone who faces battle. And that I approve of. But it is the extent of it with which I disagree. I understand officers are awarded every time they are transferred to a new city."

"I take it you do not consider defending our country worthy of praise. Perhaps you question our country's existence."

"Only two countries in the world are based on ideology – Israel and Pakistan. Our country lost its ideology, a country of Muslims, when Bangladesh seceded years ago. The economy is in shambles with no signs of improvement. Poverty is increasing. Internationally, we are known as terrorists. We survive on loans from international banks that control our sovereignty. Fifty years after inception, Pakistan is a failed state."

"What a load of rubbish!" Mona's response was immediate. "This country was made through blood and toil. We have a religion, an entity, an identity and a future more promising than half the nations of the world. The peasantry is hard working, the army loyal and the masses devoted to Islam. This is fifth-column propaganda spread by Indian intelligence and soaked up by pseudo-intellectuals living with an identity crisis of their own. All this country lacks is patriots."

The group was shocked at the unexpected outburst by the woman. Zahid noticed first her lovely deep blue eyes, then other perfectly-balanced features of her anatomy. Kamran was visibly shaken. Gathering his composure, in a low tone he offered, "I apologize for hurting your patriotism, Madam. That was not the intent."

"What is the intent of diminishing one's own country? This country nourishes us. Gives us an identity. And all we can do is find fault with it."

"Colonel Sahib, if your wife can cook half as well as she debates, you are a lucky man." Zahid's diversion was welcomed with grateful smiles from all except Mona and Kamran. Zahid looked directly at Mona. She started to reply but his gaze told her that his next sentence would embarrass her. Her eyes blinked and he could see the plea for acquittal. That was sufficient for Zahid. Turning to Colonel Javed, he inquired about plans for next month's Defence Day. The conversation turned.

Mona leaned back in her seat and stared into the flowers. Kamran saw the pain in her face and for a moment her lean body draped in blue merged with the red flowers. Her sad stillness in contrast with the gay flowers dancing in the light breeze. Never had he experienced such harmony of beauty and sadness. Picking up his tea, he wished he had never spoken.

They left shortly after. In the car Zahid said, "I'd like to top that hearty meal with a betel-leaf *paan*." They drove past the army check post, turned onto the Mall Road and into the parking lot of the Pearl Continental Hotel. A large turbaned man was stationed at the entrance to the five-star hotel. He opened the glass door with a small nod. Zahid and Kamran entered the large marbled foyer dotted with red Afghan wool and blue Persian silk carpets. To the left was a grand piano. People kept passing, oblivious to the tunes the pianist was playing. In turn, he played as if he were alone in the large hall.

A bit further down the hall a dark-skinned man of frail build sat in front of a little table covered with small brass cups full of cinnamon, parsley, mint, tobacco, sugar and limestone. Two large jars contained thick paste, one orange the other red. Wooden, long-handled spoons rested in each. On a flat plate lay a stack of green betel leaves. A couple of men and a woman watched as the dark-skinned man placed a betel leaf on his left hand. Using the spoons, he spread each of the pastes on the leaf, then with his fingers sprinkled a pinch from each of the small cups. He then folded the leaf with its contents into a cone. Picking up a small piece of newspaper he wrapped the *paan* in it. Once he had collected four of these he handed them to the waiting man, took his money and proceeded to prepare the concoction for the remaining customers.

Zahid passed the performance, took a seat at the coffee bar and waved for a waiter. Kamran followed and while sitting asked, "What about your *paan*?"

"There's a crowd. I can't stand waiting." He ordered ice cream. Kamran ordered a coffee and remained quiet. "Are you still fretting over that colonel's wife at the Mess?" Zahid asked. "She should have kept her mouth shut. Women and thinking do not go together. They should be pretty and accepting. That's all. My father wanted me to marry an educated woman. I put my foot down. I told him I would only consider women who have never set foot on a college campus. My wife has only a high school education. I am happy. She is loyal and stays at home with the children." He took a large chunk of ice cream and continued, "God, that Colonel's wife is pretty. But what does she know of the economy or how much debt the country is in? She doesn't begin to fathom the issues you were discussing."

"You are missing the point, Zahid. While I was being objective, she was patriotic. You could feel the passion. Somewhere along the line I have lost the passion. Everything must be objective and rational. Why can't we allow emotions to factor in our decision?"

"Patriotism, my foot. She should lecture her husband."

Kamran offered a blank look.

"Don't you know? Her husband was a board member of the Highway Commission. Where do you think all his wealth comes from?"

"I thought he was a landlord with an estate."

"Nobody with inheritance or money enlists in the army. Only people like me with no money join the army. When you see a senior officer with wealth you can rest assured it is ill-gotten money. The contractors pay as much as half the contract money in bribes to members of the board to secure contracts. Once the officers are bought, they approve substandard roads. After the bribes and the contractor's take there is hardly anything left to spend on the actual project. I have put in a request for transfer. In the right department, I could make a fortune in a couple of years."

"Doesn't that bother you?"

"Yes, the transfer process is cumbersome. You have to oblige a lot of people. But once in, the rewards are worth it."

"No, I mean taking bribes."

"We call it commission."

"You can call it whatever you like."

"But that's the norm. This is how army officers accumulate wealth. People accept it. Besides, in the army the procedures are well established and there is no chance of punishment or conviction. We officers are allotted houses the government builds. That is legitimate. But when the Prime Minister allocates a plot to a member of parliament, it is considered corruption. Army corruption is institutionalized. Honestly, you don't expect me to survive on my meagre salary. I couldn't even afford breakfast. Besides, parliamentarians, bureaucrats, businessmen, tax evading citizens, who in this country is not corrupt?"

"I know of honest men in all these categories. I know honest army officers. People living with the fear of God."

"You can find losers everywhere. Actually, no matter what state of mind you are in, you will always find a group of people who agree with you. I came to that realization after much contemplation." He called for the bill, placed a one hundred rupee bill on the plate and told the waiter to keep the change.

CHAPTER 9

Stepping out of the bathroom, Mona checked the clock and realized it was nearing lunchtime. She tied a rubber band around her still-wet hair and proceeded to the kitchen. She removed from the fridge two large aubergines, a pack of yoghurt and slices of pre-peeled garlic. Using a marble beater she mashed the garlic into a fine paste. She then dumped the yoghurt into a large open glass dish, added the paste, salt and a little water and battered the yoghurt. The doorbell rang and she could hear the door opening. Khadija, her neighbour, entered the kitchen with her slow waddle. "What are we up to today? Oh, my favourite. I am staying for lunch!"

"It has been a while since I cooked it. I'm all alone so I thought I would prepare this simple meal. It's good you dropped by. I was feeling lonely."

"Where were you last evening?"

"Javed took me to this dreadful ceremony at the officer's mess."

Mona placed the aubergine on the cutting plate and holding the vegetable with her right hand began cutting it into thin oval slices.

"Anything exciting?"

Mona let her shoulders drop for a moment. She looked up and then continued to slice.

"I had an argument. A civilian had come with an officer friend. I scolded the poor guy for not being patriotic."

"I hope you told him off."

"Actually, I feel sorry for him. He is one of those who go abroad and return with a foreign education full of bright ideas."

"You went abroad and returned with a foreign education."

"They either read an exciting book or some professor has lent them an idea or two and they think they can mend the world. How naive. How innocent. Like a kid with candy.

Instead of learning and understanding our society better, they are hell bound to change it, to westernize it."

Khadija poured oil in the frying pan.

"That's the trouble with education. It gives you too many ideas. You lose your bearings." Khadija complained.

"But he was genuinely concerned. Most people are indifferent to the problems of our country. We accept the status as fate. No need to change. You can deal with people receptive to new ideas. With a little work, you can change them."

"What can you change? It is the will of Allah that decides our fate. What can a human do?"

When all the slices were fried Mona quickly chopped some garlic and dumped it into the hot oil. As the garlic turned dark brown, she poured the oil over the yoghurt.

The boy servant had just entered with hot fresh bread from the bakery. He laid out the table and left. Mona carried the aubergine plate while Khadija took the yogurt. The two sat at the table and enjoyed their simple meal.

CHAPTER 10

Kamran was not enthusiastic about the trip to the Kaghan Valley. He knew the North of Pakistan was beautiful with high mountains and green valleys watered by streams from melting glaciers. But the thought of spending two days with office colleagues seemed a waste of a summer weekend. Two Toyota SUVs were parked at the UN office. Luggage was loaded and by eight o'clock they were ready to roll.

The three-hour trip to Balakot was pleasant with a well-paved double-lane asphalt road. They stopped in Balakot for tea and then began the ascent into the mountain area. The narrow unpaved road was cut out of the mountain and small streams of glacier water traversed it every few hundred meters. The vehicle was put in four-wheel drive and on occasion, rocks underneath would slip and the vehicle would swivel. The air became thinner and the driver turned the air-conditioning off. Kamran rolled down his window and breathed the fresh alpine air. Tall evergreen pine trees covered the mountain ranges. White and grey clouds hovered over the valleys beneath. Kamran could not believe that just a few hours ago he was suffering the summer heat in Islamabad.

The traffic was scarce and the narrow road often forced them to stop for oncoming traffic to pass. The sixty kilometres took them three hours before they reached the main town of Kaghan Valley. Houses were made of roughly cut wood and stone. Roofs were tapered for winter snow. Small boys in black and grey *shalwar-kameez* played in the streets. Most wore the school cap made of black felt with a red square sown on the front. Wearing their school uniform on a holiday showed the limits of their wardrobes. Girls were also visible but less in number. Most did not wear uniforms because they had no school. Some were barefoot. Others carried younger brothers and sisters. The children were skinny and looked as if their young lives had not yet experienced a warm bath. They smiled and waved at the vehicles.

The last leg of the trip was up a steep mountain. A local guide advised them to lessen the weight on each vehicle. A Willy's Jeep was hired and some luggage placed on it. Kamran and a colleague from the other vehicle jumped in. A young boy standing besides the jeep driver hopped in and smiled at Kamran. The three vehicles began their upward journey. The road had now all but disappeared. It was wide enough for a single vehicle only. Gravel stones became bigger. The streams from the mountain became larger and full stretches of the road were under water. The drivers from Islamabad were finding it difficult to control their vehicles, which kept slipping; the four-wheel drive did not amount to much.

They passed several hikers walking their way up the mountain. Kamran thought the walk was far safer than the drive. The climb became steeper and the passengers could no longer see the road ahead. All they could see was the blue sky. The Jeep slipped over a large rock and began sliding backwards. The roadside had no embankments and the valley was half a kilometre below. The driver changed gear but the vehicle kept sliding. The driver yelled, "Say the name of the Lord!" The passengers were dumbfounded and could not believe what was happening. The boy jumped out of the moving vehicle. He ran to the edge of the road, picked up a sizable rock and dropped it behind the rear right wheel. The jeep swivelled and the left wheel continued to slip. The right wheel was about to climb over the rock when the boy threw another rock behind the left wheel. The vehicle stopped and the boy jumped back into it and smiled at Kamran.

They crossed the peak and were driving downwards. Kamran could not believe his eyes. Surrounded on four sides by snow-clad mountain peaks, there was a lake the size of a small town. The driver said, "Gentlemen, welcome to the lake of beauty and mystique, Lake Saiful Maluk."

They reached the single hotel and Kamran was glad to stand on firm ground again. The shock of the travel had not worn off by the time he checked in and went to his room on the second floor. He washed his face with cold water, then stepped onto the balcony.

The lake was like a perfect cup, deep with emerald-coloured water. Two glaciers, one to the east and the other to the west, ran from the mountaintops down to the lake's lip. To the south a single small stream flowed from the lake. The mountains stood tall and firm as if guarding the enormous beauty beneath. The blue sky draped the mountain ridges. The water was so blue, the lake seemed as deep as the mountains were high. He was engulfed with a sudden desire to sail in the middle of the lake and be part of this harmony of water, land and sky.

They had a late lunch and Kamran estimated the sun would set in another hour or so. He was at the reception desk asking about next morning's breakfast timings.

"Hello." He turned to see where the voice came from. It was Mona.

"Hi."

"I would ask what you were doing here if the lake weren't so obvious."

"This is nice."

"Indeed it is. Saiful Maluk is one of the most beautiful lakes in the world."

"Absolutely beautiful."

"I am sketching outside; would you like to join me?"

"Yes, sure." Kamran turned to follow Mona. He placed his key on the reception desk. Turned and picked it up. Hesitated, then dropped it again. He went outside and saw Mona seated beside an easel with a sketch on it. An attendant brought another chair and placed it beside the small table.

"I am here with a group of my students. I teach fine arts at a college in Rawalpindi. It is a chance for the girls to enjoy the outdoors. Once they are married..."

"They belong to their husbands," Kamran added.

"Let us say they have responsibilities."

"Where is Colonel Sahib?"

"He is abroad with friends."

"On business?"

"I suppose you could say that. It is more business of lust than of commerce."

Kamran did not expect her forwardness. "I see."

"Do you? And why aren't you married? Javed told me you are still floating."

"I have studies to blame for that. I was too busy encrypting."

"Encrypting?"

"My thesis. Breaking computer codes."

Mona picked up the pencil and returned to her drawing. "That is an excuse, not a reason." The waiter arrived. "I'd like some tea; would you?"

"Yes, please. Very much indeed." After a thoughtful pause, Kamran continued, "I find it difficult to relate to people. I took a course on inter-personal skills."

Mona smiled. "I suppose you can find a course on everything nowadays."

"It did not help."

"Of course not. I was keen on studying Allama Iqbal. Iqbaliyat they call it. But I found him..."

"Over-rated?"

"Yes. Precisely."

"Then you and I are in a minority. I can't say this without inviting a fight.

Mostly from people who have never read the man."

"Anyhow, I turned to fine arts. It is nice. I like sculpting. But in our society, figures of the human body are not appreciated. So I paint landscapes."

"At times our conservatism amazes me."

"It is the fabric of our society. Don't go against it. Accept it."

The tea arrived. Kamran politely waved the waiter away and poured the tea.

Mona had sketched the mountains and the lake. She was now drawing the stream.

Finishing her tea, she said "I want to feel the water." She took her sandals off and walked barefoot on the grass towards the stream. She turned back and asked, "Coming?"

Kamran hesitated and followed with his shoes on. She tied her *dupatta* behind her back and finding a stable, flat rock sat on it, slightly pulling her *shalwar* up and placing her feet in the icy cold water. Kamran found a nearby rock and sat on it, keeping his feet dry. She turned to him and saw his reluctance. She smiled, then removed her hair band and let the breeze through her long thick hair. The sun was setting. A local woman arrived at the opposite side of the stream. She wore a long thick black and red dress with a headgear covering her hair. She carried a round earth pot. Bending down, in one sweep she filled the pot, placed it on her head and returned to where she had come from.

"You see that woman there. How lucky she is to live in such a serene place. But she has never in her life freed her hair to feel the breeze. What a crime."

"Her husband or brother or father would kill her if she did."

Raising her eyebrows with a deep breath, Mona said confidently, "She has to conform. There are certain expectations of her."

"But where do they draw the line? When do you rebel?" asked Kamran.
Turning to Kamran with a slight shake of her head, "You don't. Society has its rights over an individual. You play your assigned role." Looking down at the water "You endure."

***

It sounded like a mountain exploding. Kamran jumped out of his bed thinking for a fleeting moment that the bugle of doomsday had just been blown. Perched on the windowsill was a large rooster looking into Kamran's room. The window was left open for the fresh breeze and the rooster was taking advantage of this oversight. Puffing his wings, he repeated his morning call with the same intensity that had so abruptly interrupted the unsuspecting guest's sleep. Kamran looked into his eyes and saw no compassion, not even the slightest regret.

Instead he read duty, blatant courage and utter stupidity all mixed up.

He tried to shoo the bird away but with no impact. It was as if the rooster knew Kamran could do no harm from inside the room. As he began his third crow, Kamran opened the door and attacked the beast with a karate kick. The victim jumped onto the balcony railing, then leaped down fluttering its wings till he landed on the lawn two stories below. He ran to the nearby fountain, hopped on the brim and continued his interrupted wakeup call. Duty first.

Kamran returned to his room, sat on the bed and glanced at the clock. It was 5 a.m. Unable to sleep again, he put on a t-shirt, sport shorts and joggers and went downstairs. He passed the receptionist with a smile but got an uninterested nod in response. He continued down the foyer and noticed that the maid cleaning the glass door gave him a disapproving glance. He quickly realized his mistake, returned to his room and changed his shorts for a full-length jogging trouser. The receptionist beamed a bright smile.

Kamran took a short path behind the hotel, which led him to a grass lawn the size of a small football field. It was that early morning time just before dawn when the night had ended but light had not yet broken. The grass was wet with morning dew. After a short walk on the perimeter, he began jogging. He counted twenty laps, and on the final lap he increased his pace to a run. He was still panting when he stopped to look up at the mountain. He could see the first ray of light through the trees on the mountaintop. Kamran walked to the front garden and saw two women pacing. Recognizing Mona, he walked towards them.

"Obesity is a big problem in the West," the other woman was saying. "They just won't walk. They take their cars everywhere. How do you manage to stay fit, Mona?"

"I don't know. Nothing in particular. I really think some bodies tend to be fat, others lean. Though I do drink plenty of water with my food."

"That's enough exercise for one day. See you later." Her friend returned to the hotel. As she passed Kamran, she greeted him with a shy smile and a nod.

"I didn't imagine you as a morning person, Mr. Kamran."

"I am not. Today was an exception. For exercise, I normally play squash, in the evenings."

"In Islamabad?"

"No. In Rawalpindi, at the army courts in 10th Corps. The only courts worthy of playing at in Islamabad are the navy courts and the ones at the Presidency. I don't know anybody in the navy and the president doesn't really know me."

"Join me." Kamran continued the walk from where her friend had left. "She is a colleague. Divorced, poor thing. She loved a man in her neighbourhood but was wed to a cousin. It didn't work. She is very intelligent, and sensitive. Her family blames her for not making it work. Her heart was somewhere else."

"Our society behaves as if love doesn't exist."

"Love? Our society behaves as if lust doesn't exist."
Kamran was taken aback by her frankness. She stopped and turned to him. "Don't blush. I don't talk to everybody like this."

"That is a relief." They both laughed, continuing their walk.

"So have you had your heart broken?"

"No. But…" Kamran hesitated. They came upon a bench and sat down.

"At university in the UK, there was a fellow student", Mona said. "He was very kind to me, offering advice and information whenever possible. He insisted on driving me all the way from Manchester to Heathrow airport."

"I would think he liked you very much. Perhaps even loved you", said Kamran.

"Yes. I didn't really get to know him. Now I think, perhaps I should have. We only live once."

"To answer your question, a woman I knew. Well, she was a colleague. Very fond of samosas."

"Samosas!" Mona laughed, clapping her hands and leaning back on the bench. "Tell me more."

"She'd insist that I order them every day for tea."

Amused and enjoying every bit of this, Mona urged him to continue. "Is that all she wanted?"

"One day, she said to me 'I love you.'" Mona was now serious.

"And what was your response?" she asked.

Kamran looked at her sadly. "We went out for some time."

"Did she ask for marriage?"

"Yes."

"Then?"

"Then."

"Did you reject her?"

"I suppose you could say that."

"Why?"

Kamran looked away. His eyes were fluttering. He shook his head. "I don't know. I guess I didn't understand what it meant to be loved."

"Do you now?"

Slowly, he replied, "Yes. But I guess it is too late."

"What did you do?"

"I wrote a poem."

"A poem. After ditching a girl, you wrote a poem. Men are impossible." Playfully she said, "Let me hear it."

"No. You'll make fun."

"I probably will."

Kamran bit his lip and with a smile said, "You are the only one to hear this."

"Thanks for the utmost of privileges. Now on with the recitation. I am starving and want breakfast."

Kamran began,

"Nights have passed and days have gone
Her words still ring my ears
You broke my heart

"She didn't fight
She didn't scream
She didn't cuss, curse or demean
With tears in her eyes
She wept, You broke my heart

"If she'd complained
I could have explained
The ten reasons I had to change

"She did not accuse

INTERNAL AFFAIRS — Asif Niazi

She did not abuse
There was no exchange
But what she said, You broke my heart

"Time has passed
The days have lapsed
My reasons failed and wandered
The pain lingers in those words
You broke my heart

"Let her be
For a heart once broken can not mend
I shall live the life of guilt
For I am the one who broke a heart

"But may my life save another
Break not what matters most
With tender love and coast
Cherish the hearts that love you dear
A life worth living is one that claims
There is not a soul that complains
You broke my heart"

"How touching. But your timing sucks." Extending her arms out, looking across to Kamran, "I am famished. I would love a *paratha*. Would you like a *paratha*?"

Thinking that eating the heavy *paratha* would undo all the exercise he had this morning, Kamran winced. Then, looking straight into her blue eyes, "I would love it."

CHAPTER 11

Zahid had an early breakfast. He stepped outside on the porch to inspect his car. The batman had already washed and dried it.

"Did you check the oil and water?" Zahid asked.

"Yes, sir. Sir, when will you be returning, sir?"

"Monday evening. Inshallah."

"Inshallah, sir."

Zahid went back in and returned with a small travel bag and two boxes of sweets he had bought last night. He placed the luggage in the trunk and drove away. On the main road, he followed the sign for Lahore and in a few minutes was on the highway. In four hours of driving, he crossed two major bridges spanning the Chenab and Jehlum rivers. Before reaching the bridge for Ravi River, he exited east to a narrow single-lane road.

The road was paved for the next hour's drive. There were fields on either side, scattered with individual houses, mostly made of mud but with an occasional brick house. The flat terrain with no mountain in sight reminded him of "the vast plains of the Punjab," a phrase he had read in an 18th century journal written by a British officer. He could see unveiled women carrying food for their men working in the fields.

The paved road now ended into a dirt road. Reducing speed, Zahid manoeuvred the road with caution. The sun was high in the sky. His vehicle was raising a lot of dust. He rolled the windows up and turned the air-conditioning on. He crossed two small bridges and then drove along a canal with paved embankments. After two kilometres, he took a sharp left and entered the village boundary. He drove up to a house with thick mud walls and a small wooden door.

INTERNAL AFFAIRS   Asif Niazi

The door was open. A bamboo curtain hung in the door. Zahid parked the car, opened the trunk and entered the house without knocking. Inside was a large courtyard with rooms at the far end. There was a water tap to the right side. A few washed dishes were lying on a *charpoy*. A woman was sitting on a low wooden stool churning yogurt. To the left was a wide verandah with a roof of hay. A large black buffalo stood munching on fresh grass. A couple of children sitting near the woman ran to Zahid and greeted him. The woman rose and placing her *dupatta* on her head greeted him, "Salam, Sahib."

"Hello, Khairaan. Is all well?"

"Yes Sahib, with the grace of Allah."

Zahid offered a weak handshake to the children and asked them to fetch the luggage. He crossed the courtyard. An old, frail man emerged from the room. He wore thick horn-rimmed glasses and a sleeveless white shirt with large pockets. Around his waist was wrapped a blue and white *dhoti* cloth that ended between his knee and ankles. As he walked, the *dhoti* revealed his legs. His teeth were rich with tobacco stains. The old man smiled and with raised arms embraced Zahid.

"What a nice day! My son has arrived. Did you have any trouble on the way?"

"No, Da Ji. My journey was fine, except for the heat and dust."

"Son, dust is what makes our bodies and heat is what drives us. Come inside."

The room was a rectangle. Along the left, short wall was a *charpoy* with two large pillows. There were no sheets or bedding on the *charpoy*. At the other end of the room, the floor was covered with yellow and bright blue vinyl mats. Cotton sheets with large pillows were spread over the mats. The ceiling was high and made of wooden beams holding hay. In the centre dropped a ceiling fan, originally painted white but now yellow with age. It slowly twirled with a small squeak.

Zahid's father sat on the *charpoy* with large pillows. Zahid's stepmother, who was only a few years older than Zahid, greeted him followed by his widowed aunt and his two young stepsisters. Zahid sat at the feet of the *charpoy*. Pulling his *hookah* nearer, Da Ji put the long pipe in his mouth and took a deep breath. The *hookah* made a bubbling sound.

After a brief chat, Zahid left to bathe before lunch. The only plumbing in the bathroom was a single cold water tap at knee height. Zahid mused at the crudity of rural life. The cool bath left him feeling clean and fresh. Lunch was simple, with chicken, spinach, yoghurt and lots of cool *lassi*.

"Take a nap, son. In the evening, when the heat has lessened, we will pay our respects to Chowdhry Sahib."

"Da Ji, I have said this before. Why do I have to pay respects to the Chowdhrys? They give us nothing. I have an independent income. We do not depend on them."

"This is a tradition of our forefathers."

"Father, our family is more educated than the Chowdhrys. I live in the city. I am a commissioned officer in the Pakistan army. What did the Chowdhrys do to earn their lands, connive with the British?"

"Son, they are still the protectors of the village. They set the law. They hold secrets. They decide which family is respectable and which is low. When armed men raided our lands, who stood by your grandfather defending our property? It was the Chowdhry's men."

"But they were serving their own interests."

"We all serve our own interests. If not for them, your grandfather and his sons would have been slain and..."

"But father…"

"…and our women disgraced. Hold your tongue and honour those who protect our honour. While you roam the city in your fancy car and uniform, who protects our women in the village? Certainly not you. And have you heard what your brother has done?"

"No. Is he all right?"

"He ran away from medical college. He joined the religious *tablighis*. He now roams villages inviting people to Islam, as if they were not Muslims to begin with."

"That can not be."

"Oh yes. Eighteen years of schooling. Two more years to become a doctor. The first doctor in our whole community. And he throws all that away for something he could have done with no schooling at all. What a waste. I should have listened to your dead mother, sending him to school was a waste. A total waste. As a result of that time at school, he knows nothing of farming. He can't tell if a seed is ripe or raw. He can't milk a cow, weave a basket or manage the plough. He can't water the fields or market any of our produce. All he does is lecture me on religion."

"But why?"

"It is not only him. Others are doing the same. Two of Fida's sons have gone the same way. Ask your schoolmaster friend." Zahid was visibly disturbed. He went to the next room, turned the fan on and lay on a *charpoy* deep in thought.

Following their afternoon tea, Zahid and his father set off to the Chowdhrys' mansion. Once there, the walk from the main gate to the living quarters took five minutes. Both sides of the path were covered with orchards of orange and mango trees. Chowdhry Sahib was holding court on one of his lawns. Wearing all white and a large turban on his head, he was half-lying on a massive *charpoy*, a big pillow under his right arm. Two male servants, sitting on their haunches, were massaging Chowdhry Sahib's feet. An elegant walking stick with a white ebony handle and dark wood shaft hung from the *charpoy's* foot. By the looks of Chowdhry Sahib's health, the stick was more for appearance than for support.

Chowdhry Sahib slowly drew on a brightly-coloured *hookah*. Red, boat-shaped sandals with gold-coloured embroidery were on the grass. A man with thick spectacles holding a large ledger book sat on a chair to his right. In front, about two dozen men sat on the grass listening to him. Women petitioners formed a smaller group sitting on the grass at a distance. They were swarmed by children. Three large men stood behind his *charpoy*. Two were armed with large staves while the third wore a machine gun on his shoulder. Chowdhry Sahib had proclaimed judgment on the last case when the two arrived.

"Welcome Mian Sahib. I see you have brought your son with you today."

"Salam, Chowdhry Sahib." Zahid's father knelt low and touched the Chowdhry's feet. Zahid made a similar gesture but did not touch. Chowdhry motioned them to sit on a *charpoy* to his left, the side at which his feet were, indicative of their status. He dismissed the assembly and turned to Mian Sahib and his son.

"What news of the city do you bring, son?"

"Nothing new. The military government is promising elections."

"Remember, son. Whether the government is civilian or military, the real power remains with the military. That is how it has been for centuries. I personally do not like this democracy vulgarity. My servants, people who feed off my land, have the same vote as I. Preposterous. This reminds me," he said, turning to the man with the ledger, "that son of the cobbler, the one who joined the army, I hear he returned to the village but did not visit us."

"That is correct, Chowdhry Sahib. He has been here three days."

"What about the well that his father has charge of? Is he taking good care of it?"

"Yes, Chowdhry Sahib, he is."

"He is not. On the other hand, our gardener, Juma Din, who has no sons, is loyal and has come across some bad luck of late. His crops have failed. Send word that he is to take over responsibility of the well from the cobbler. He is also to collect revenue from the well."

"As you wish, Chowdhry Sahib."

"And is that Master Ji still running his school after I had warned him?"

"Yes Sahib, he is. But since he has no longer any place, he teaches in the open air, under the banyan tree."

"A stubborn man he is. Mian Sahib, what does your third son do?"

"He is a director at the Water Department of the Ministry of Environment.

He enforces water purification regulations."

Not understanding, one masseur whispered to his partner, "What does he do?" On getting a reply, he frowned with confusion, thought for a moment, then exclaimed, "I get it. He just searches for bugs in water."

"Something like that."

Zahid cleared his throat and said, "Chowdhry Sahib, all Master Ji does is teach. It is a service to the community."

With a small laugh, Chowdhry Sahib shifted to an upright position, waving away the masseurs. He drew on his *hookah* and while exhaling smoke said, "Son, your profession and mine are similar. We landlords in the village and you military officers in the cities, we both thrive on large numbers of illiterate men. To us education is cancer. But being illiterate, I cannot be blamed for not supporting education. What is the military's excuse? Remember, restricting funds for education has been a policy of this country's rulers for the last fifty years. Whose interest does this policy serve?" Turning to Zahid's father, he said, "It was nice of you to come. Stay for dinner."

"Thank you, Chowdhry Sahib. But we must be leaving for home now. God bless."

***

The next day Zahid had a faulty table fan placed in the car. Crossing the courtyard, he told Khairaan, "I will drop this off at the repair shop and then visit Master Ji." The shop was a narrow tunnel hardly four feet wide with used fans and old fan parts displayed everywhere. The technician was a young man assisted by a boy hardly eight years old.

"Salam, Mian Sahib," the technician greeted Zahid. "You could have sent word. I would have collected the fan myself."

"I was coming in this direction anyway. Could you write me a receipt?"

The technician nodded hesitantly, turned around and opened the drawer of a battered desk. The desktop had a solder gun, some screws and a few screwdrivers on it. "I do not have paper, Sahib Ji."

Zahid pulled a piece of paper out of his wallet and gave it to the technician.

"Would you have a pen, Sahib Ji?"

"What is the matter? Why are you not equipped?" Zahid asked.

"I have no need for pen and paper, Sahib Ji. I am illiterate. So is this boy. Perhaps you would have a pen in your car. You may write the receipt there."

Zahid returned to the car annoyed. He fetched a pen from the glove compartment and began to write but stopped with a shake of his head. He looked back at the shop where the technician had already unscrewed the fan top. Crumpling the paper, he drove off.

The road rose slightly and after crossing a short wooden bridge, he turned left towards a very large banyan tree. A man stood there with a small cane in his hand. Five boys and two girls sat in front of him on two rows of straw mats. The children were writing on small wooden tablets with pens made of bamboo shoot. The teacher would dictate and the children would dip their pens in the pots and write on the tablets. Seeing Zahid approach, Master Ji told the class to read. They picked up their *qaeda* booklets. Master Ji gave Zahid a big hug and led him to a *charpoy* placed in the shade under the tree.

"You bastard," mocked Master Ji.

"You good for nothing fool," returned Zahid.

"Where the hell have you been all this time? Are you still with Military Intelligence?"

Zahid quickly looked around to see if anyone could hear. The children had dropped their *qaedas*. The girls were chatting. Two boys pulled marbles out of their pockets and began playing. A third pulled out a slingshot and picking up a few pebbles walked around the tree searching for birds.

"Yes I am. But I have put in for a transfer."

"That is what you said the last time we met."

"You know how these things work. Enough of me. What happened to the school?"

"Chowdhry repossessed it."

"But didn't it belong to the government?"

"No. Chowdhry had lent the property to the Ministry of Education. The government never built a school for our village. The government appointed Ama Noori's son as the District Education Officer. Chowdhry could not stand it so he kicked us out. I have hopes he will change his mind. Otherwise, by next month it would be too hot to continue."

"He should be shot."

"He is not the problem. People with education do not stay in the village. They shift, like you have, to the cities leaving illiterates to be ruled by a Chowdhry. Those with even more education leave the cities and live in Western countries. It is a process you can't fight. Our country doesn't want educated people. The whole system is geared to get rid of us."

"Oh shut up. Tell me, when are you going for Haj pilgrimage?"

"It is not in my stars."

"You are not doing well, my friend." Pointing to the mats below and the tree above, he said, "Look at you. You call this a school?"

"A school is an institution where learning takes place. The children actually do learn here."

"No floor, no roof. Desk, chair, filing cabinet, you have nothing."

"Ah. To you an institution is a building with paper in it. Ours is a verbal society. We cannot read, therefore there is nothing to write. In a verbal society, individuals are institutions. Chowdhry Sahib is an institution. No paper work. But an institution in every right."

"I think a few more months under this banyan tree and you will become completely insane. Come to the city and lead a decent life."

"Some of the most beautiful lessons of life originated from people meditating under a tree."

Zahid shook his head in desperation.

Three young bearded men approached. They wore white dresses with the *shalwar* cut short so that their ankles were visible. They wore white hats on their heads. One was Zahid's younger brother.

"*Assalamulaikum.*" They greeted Zahid and Master Ji, who returned the greeting. Zahid hugged his brother and shook hands with the other two. He motioned them to sit.

"Da Ji told me you arrived yesterday."

"Yes, where were you?"

"We were on a missionary trip to the neighbouring village." He pulled out a rosary from his pocket and began to whisper as he shifted the beads.

Zahid was abrupt: "What has happened to you? Is it true you have left medical school?" Running his right hand down his beard, Zahid's brother said, "The world is coming to an end. There is corruption everywhere. No values. The word of Allah is what matters. People have gone astray. They need guidance."

"The village needs a doctor."

"There are no jobs. We have graduate doctors working as delivery boys for pharmaceutical companies. Unless you are corrupt you cannot earn a living. The system is corrupt. It must be changed. To change, we must first change our behaviour."

"The first step is education."

Another *tablighi* said politely, "I beg your pardon. I wish to put a question to you." The man, in his early twenties, had a sparkle in his eyes.

"Yes, go ahead," Zahid replied.

"You speak of education." Motioning towards the teacher, he continued, "Master Ji is amongst us today. Tell me, of what good is education?"

Zahid smiled at this simple question but before he could reply the young man continued, "Our government is composed of educated people. Is it not?" Zahid nodded but could not fathom where this conversation was going. "What good does the government do for its people? Our leaders fail us because they lack not knowledge but character. What I am saying is, what good is education when it does not build character?"

Zahid sighed and looking at Master Ji said with desperation, "I will be leaving tomorrow, thank God."

His brother pointed towards the nearby mosque. "It is prayer time. We are going to the mosque. Come with us, brothers."

Master Ji replied, "You brothers go ahead."

"We will pray for you."

"Please do. God bless you."

***

That evening Zahid had dinner at Master Ji's house. They sat on wooden chairs in the courtyard. Dinner was served on a small wooden table. Master Ji's three-year-old son sat on his lap eating with his father. The other children were indoors eating with the women. Master Ji cleared the table before his wife and mother joined them. Master Ji offered Zahid a pillow to lean on and said, "According to the constitution, your military bosses who ordered the coup are guilty of high treason punishable by death."

Collecting the dishes, his wife commented, "Let him be, Master Ji. Junior officers and soldiers are merely following orders. You can't expect Zahid Bhai to explain the actions of his seniors."

Downing his glass of *lassi,* Zahid replied, "Who cares what the constitution says? It is a piece of paper. Paper can be torn anytime. Do you care?" Placing his empty glass on the tray, he said, "Thank you Bhabi." The hostess took the dishes and returned with tea.

Master Ji continued, "We in villages have a different take. We don't hold the constitution dear. It was copied from other places. It does not reflect our values. Let me explain." Turning to his mother, he asked, "Ma Ji. What is the biggest crime of all?"

"Son, why must you involve me in your discussions? I am a simple villager. Murder, theft, deceit all are crimes in the eyes of the Lord."

Master Ji continued, "What did Chowdhry Ilahi do to Lal Din?"

Upon hearing this, his mother raised her *dupatta* and covered her mouth. Waiving her hand, she told Zahid, "Son, I have seven sons and one daughter. I am willing to sacrifice all my sons for the honour of my daughter. That is what sons are for. To protect the honour of their mother and sisters. I can live in poverty. Without cars, bungalows, electricity. But I can't live in shame. I'd rather die than live in shame. Chowdhry Ilahi abducted Lal Din's unmarried teenage daughter. In our village, in our society, that is the ultimate crime one can commit. No punishment is enough for the perpetrator of this crime. In our society, it is the ultimate crime. There are no two opinions about it."

Master Ji, with the air of an attorney who had just proven a major point, intervened. "Now tell me where," opening both arms, "does this crime stand in our constitution?" Zahid was not amused and with a nod continued with his tea.

"You villagers sure know how to eat. I am stuffed."

"Let's take a walk." The two left the house and took a narrow lane towards the canal. It was dark with little light from the half moon. Zahid was walking with difficulty on the uneven road. There were no streetlights. Master Ji trod confidently. As they got further from the houses, Master Ji asked, "What do you know about the conspiracy theory?"

"The what?"

"Conspiracy theory."

"What conspiracy? Against whom?"

"Is everybody at the Military Intelligence as daft as you? Minutes of a secret meeting of the corp commanders have been leaked. This was the meeting last year that decided to overthrow the then civilian government. According to rumour, the officers discussed why the action was necessary. Statistics were presented showing the army needed to increase its budget."

"The army is always in need of budget. Our enemy, India, has ten times more military power. What else is new?"

"The meeting considered military expenses of last year."

"So?"

"Including how much was spent on officers' welfare."

"No big deal."

"How much commission was made on last year's tank deal. The revenue collected from sale of land mines to Tamil rebels and foreign bank balances of retired generals."

This made Zahid stop. He looked around and, holding his friend's hand, spoke earnestly. "Ijaz, you are dealing with fire. Tell me the source of this information and do not mention this subject again. Not with anybody."

"So you do know about it."

"Only that there is a high-level inquiry on the leak. Whoever are responsible will regret for the rest of their short lives. This is a matter of national security."

"Which part? The commissions or the money stashed away in foreign bank accounts?"

"They will spare no one. Once caught, they will be tortured at the Attock Fort. They will either rot there for the rest of their lives or face summary executions. No trials. This is catastrophic. If the public ever came to know what amounts of money we are talking about, there would be riots everywhere. Those idiots should never have compiled such statistics."

"But surely the generals must have requested such data."

"The rift in the army between fundamentalists and pro-Westerners has reached a dangerous level. There are Islamic fundamentalists at every level of the army, even generals. It is that damn Afghanistan war that is haunting us. The fundis want to leak this information to disgrace the ruling junta."

"But what significance is an annual report?"

Zahid walked up the canal bank and stood beside the tube-well. Master Ji followed. Noise from the running water and engine made it impossible for anyone to overhear them.

"It is much more. It covers times since the first military coup, the three wars with India, the four coups and the Afghan and Kargil wars. It is one of the most authentic documents compiled by the military. Every major military purchase: aircraft, tanks, submarines and the paybacks involved, the fortunes amassed and the extravagance of senior officers. It is damning information. God help us if it ever surfaces."

CHAPTER 12

As Mona finished her evening prayers, Khadija arrived at Mona's house with Sabina. Khadija said, "This girl just has to go shopping tonight. And she insists we go together."

"What a good idea. Sabina, go fetch Marina."

Sabina went to Marina's room. "Fabric for summer dresses is on display at Gul's. Want to come?"

Marina grabbed her *dupatta* and following Sabina jumped into the back of Mona's car. Khadija took the front passenger seat. Mona pulled the car out onto the street and proceeded west on Mall Road. At a busy intersection she turned right, passed the post office and took a left, reaching the main Saddar bazaar street.

The road was wide but crowded. Cars, motorbikes and pedestrians mingled. Street hawkers were selling popcorn, ice cream, cassettes, prayer hats, belts, and picture posters. Young boys and girls were visiting parked cars asking for money. Sabina pointed to a vacant space into which Mona pulled quickly. To their right a green Army jeep was parked. The driver, a soldier in uniform, was standing besides the vehicle observing the shopping spree.

The four walked a short distance to Gul's fabric house. The shop was well lit. There were mannequins displaying cotton fabrics designed for the summer heat. There were mostly light colours of yellow, pink and blue covered with coloured flowers. The mannequins wore long and short-sleeve shirts with long *dupattas*.

The girls proceeded directly to the cotton section. The attendant began pulling reams of fabric from the cupboards behind him, unfolding and laying the fabric on the counter in front. Sabina kept feeling the fabric with her fingers and selected a length of pink cloth with small flowers. The flowers were slightly darker than the fabric base. She placed her hand under the thin cloth and could almost see through. She glanced at Marina, who flashed a disapproving look. "Too revealing".

Sabina blushed and looking back at the attendant said, "Is this breadth one metre or a metre and a quarter?"

"A metre and a quarter, Ba Ji. A full dress would require five meters length."

"Fine. Cut it. Thanks." The attendant picked up the metre rod and placing it along the cloth began wrapping the cloth along the length of the rod. He measured the fifth round, added a few more inches and cut a few inches into the fabric along its width with his scissors. He then held the ends in each hand and pulled. The cut ran along the width of the cloth and separated the piece from the roll. He folded the piece and placing it in a plastic bag said, "You can find a matching *dupatta* at the other counter."

Sabina selected another two lengths of cloth. Marina settled for a single thick piece of dark blue. As they were turning toward the *dupatta* section, two girls approached the counter. One spoke with the attendant, then turned to her sister and began signing with her hands. She pointed to the flowers on the fabric and with a frown opened her fingers. Her sister nodded. The sister then said, "I need the same color but with smaller flowers."

Khadija and Mona each paid for her daughter's shopping. As they left the shop, Sabina asked Marina, "Did you see that poor deaf girl?"

"It is the will of God. In this disability there must be some higher meaning."

"I wonder if there could be some cure for it."

"It is the will of God. You can't do anything about it."

"Sure you can. Modern science can do wonders."

"You can not alter the will of God. That is the way God created her and that is the way He intended."

"Sure you can. I bet if she were in some Western country, they would have fixed her disability."

"You can't fight destiny."

"We make our own destiny."

"God makes destiny. Without God's will you couldn't even take a step." Sabina could see how serious Marina was getting. Taking a long step forward, she said "You mean like this." Taking another step "or this" and then another "or this," she ran to the car with Marina following her. As they all sat in the car, Marina complained, "Mama, Sabina is making fun of God."

Sabina replied quickly, "You are twisting the story. I was teasing you."

Turning to her mother, she said, "Mama, Marina thinks she is God."

Khadija protested, saying "What rubbish. May God have mercy."

Sabina appealed to Mona. "Aunti, I was just saying we craft our own destiny, and Marina claims everything is the will of God."

Marina replied, "Our lives are pre-ordained. We can't change anything."

Mona laughed and turning to Khadija said, "The battle of Ibn Rushd and Imam Ghazali."

"Have fear of Allah, Mona. The sky will fall down. Equating these two with those holy men."

"Who were they, Mama?" asked Marina.

"They were Muslim scholars. They interpreted our religion in different ways."

"What ways, Aunti?"

"Ibn Rushd, known as Averroes in the West, taught that according to Islam, we can shape our destiny. Therefore we are accountable for our actions." She took a right turn.

"That sounds pretty reasonable, Aunti."

"What did Imam Ghazali teach, Mama?"

"He believed that according to Islam, everything that happens is the will of God. We can not alter what God has pre-ordained." They stopped at a red light.

"He was right, Mama."

Sabina turned to her mother "Who was right, Mama?"

"You'd better ask Mona, dear. I don't understand these intellectual arguments. What I know is what I was taught by my elders. A bird can not flap a wing without the will of God." Marina felt satisfied. "Mama, tell Sabina who is right."

"Actually, both." The light turned green and Mona accelerated. "We must decide and behave as if our decision affects the outcome. That is our obligation and responsibility. In a larger context, all that happens is the will of God. The West adopted Ibn Rushd's interpretations. Muslims, by and large, adhere to Imam Ghazali." After a pause, as if speaking to herself, "Free will is overrated."

"What?" asked Khadija.

"Our actions are based on our decisions. The decisions are based on our nature and knowledge. These in turn are based on experiences and stimuli. Where is the room for free will?"

Khadija turned her focus to the chaos in traffic.

CHAPTER 13

The Intelligence Branch conference hall was in a single-story colonial-era structure, not far from the main entrance to the Army General Headquarters in Rawalpindi. With its red shingled rooftop and wide corridors, it blended in with other surrounding offices.

At 9:20, a car with security vehicles pulled in front of the conference hall. The soldier on guard quickly opened the rear door. General Zewar Beg emerged wearing light brown sunglasses. He carried a short cane. He wore the standard khaki uniform with pea cap, a broad brass-buckle belt and shining black shoes. Except for the epaulettes and stars his uniform was similar to those of the officers and soldiers assembled to greet him. Of middle age and middle stature, he carried himself with terrifying confidence that separated him from the others.

The group saluted the general, who made a slight but firm motion to proceed. They entered the building and through a short corridor entered the Conference room. It had a large, oblong teakwood table in the centre surrounded by twenty well-cushioned black leather executive chairs. The windows were draped by heavy curtains so that none of the bright sunlight outside could penetrate. The officers were standing and saluted as Beg arrived and took his seat at the head of the table. Without uttering a word, he motioned others to be seated.

The projector at the far end displayed the last slide of a presentation. Brigadier Arif informed the general that the detailed security presentation had just been completed and asked if he would like it to be repeated. The general said to forgo the presentation and continue with the summary.

Zahid sat at the opposite side from the general and observed his every move in detail. This was Zahid's first meeting in this forum and he wanted to make a good impression. There was only one other major in the room. He sat beside Zahid. The others were colonels and brigadiers. The colonels sat near Zahid and the brigadiers nearer to the general. Arif nodded to the officers and each, in order, covered his specialty.

As the briefing proceeded, General Beg leaned back in his chair, placed his elbows on the arms, raised his hands and began tapping his fingertips together. He continued this slowly and deliberately. The spooky atmosphere became more dreadful with each passing minute.

"Arrangements have been completed for the early retirement of Justice Shah," reported one brigadier. "His replacement was approved in our last meeting and the decision has been conveyed to the Prime Minister's office and our parliamentarians."

His colleague to the left continued, "Decision on the Education Ministry's request for more schools has been deferred for two years citing budgetary restrictions."

The next officer continued, "Sir, media is calm. Briefs and columns for the next week have been sent to the newspapers and no untoward article is expected to be published. The editor of Azad newspaper was…" He hesitated and looked at Brigadier Arif who motioned his support to continue. "…was brought in line for his article criticizing the army rule." The General nodded.

It was Zahid's turn and looking at Arif, he hesitantly asked in a low voice, "Shouldn't the education ministry request be accepted? Our illiteracy levels are rising."

The general looked at Arif who gave a sharp look at Zahid and then, turning to the General, said, "Major Zahid is new to the forum, sir." He motioned for the next officer to continue.

"Inspector General of Police was summoned to GHQ in relation to the Chandni Chowk incident."

Arif asked what the incident was.

"A traffic constable stopped General Akbar's vehicle and told the driver tinted glass windows were illegal. Of course they are illegal but this was an army general's vehicle. The driver told him whose car it was but the insolent constable was relentless. The constable is now suspended and in jail. He was given a good thrashing. At the time General Akbar was in the car.."

The general interrupted with a curt "Arif." The officers tensed. After a pause, the general asked, "Why don't you answer the major's question about education?"

Arif was unrattled. "Sir, these Ministry people are always asking for money. They can't even run the schools they have." Turning to the group for support, from the side of his mouth he said, "These bloody civilians." There were vigorous nods and murmurs of "bloody civilians" from the group. Arif began to continue, but the general interrupted. Moving forward in his seat and looking directly at Zahid, he said, "Major...", with his left hand beckoning for a name.

Arif blurted "Zahid, sir, he is new."

"Yes," continued the General. Then returning to his original position, he spoke deliberately. "Pakistan army is strong. We must know what keeps the army strong. For recruits we need a large number of illiterate jobless men. What does education achieve? A few years of education and they start asking for weird things like rights." The group nodded. "...and democracy." The group was now openly supporting and cheering the general. "Remember, young man, the army is strong because the judiciary, police, education, health, media and parliament are weak. And that is how it must stay. Understood?"

Zahid swallowed and managed to say, "Yes, sir." He could feel he made more enemies today than in his whole career; what was to have been an opportunity to impress senior officers had turned into a nightmare.

His face flushed, and he wished the wretched day had never started.

There was a slight knock on the door and it opened. Four waiters entered with trays of tea and confectionaries fresh from the Rahmat Bakery. There were thermoses of tea and coffee, freshly prepared chicken sandwiches, patties and pastries.

Beg concluded, "That will be all, gentlemen." He rose. All present rose and saluted the general. He left. The officers remained and enjoyed their tea. Zahid left without a word.

CHAPTER 14

Mona was whispering and giggling on the phone. She held it in her left hand and was playing with her hair with the other when Khadija walked in. "I have to go now," she said urgently. "Bye."

With her slow waddle, Khadija managed herself to the sofa and as she sat inquired casually, "Who was that?"

Mona was in high spirits. Walking towards Khadija, she raised both arms and adjusted her hair. "That was someone interested in buying our house. The one on the Peshawar road."

"Well?"

Sitting down "Well, what?"

"Will he buy it?"

"Oh, no. No. I once told you of a guy I scolded at the mess."

Khadija now straightened up. "I remember. Is he married?"

Mona deflected her look and with a smile. "No."

Khadija was jolted out of her walk fatigue and seemed geared up to fight a bear. With a frown: "What does he want?" Her tone indicated she was telling rather than asking a question. Sitting, Mona closed her knees tight and covered them with her hands. Avoiding eye contact, she spoke hesitantly. "He wants to learn how to paint." Looking at Khadija for a moment, she averted her eyes and stared deep into the coffee table as if she had seen a snake.

Khadija did not budge. She made no move at all. Her gaze fixed on Mona. Finally, Mona dared a look at her friend, saying, "Calm down. You are making me nervous." She stood up and began walking away.

"You make me worry. Come sit down, here." Mona returned and sat deep into the sofa, smiling. Khadija looked straight into her eyes with a stern face Mona had never before seen. "Are you in love with him?"

Mona blushed with anger and got up. "No. Of course not. What a thing to say." She walked away, then turned. Raising her hand to her forehead, she stepped back towards Khadija. "He makes me laugh."

"Oh."

"Javed is away all the time. I have no one to talk to."

Khadija was merciless. "Get a parrot." She rose and walked toward her friend. The two saw fear in each other's eyes. Mona's lips began to tremble. Her eyes watered.

"How far has this gone?"

"Khadija, you know me."

"Humans can falter any time. Especially women."

Mona sighed, raising her eyes. "He is just a friend."

"Look, girl. You are beautiful, intelligent, educated. Get a hold of yourself. That's the trouble with education. It gives you too many ideas. You lose bearings."

"That's what I like about him. He is drowning in ideas with innocence. He tries to rid the world of its problems. How naïve."

"My God, your teenage daughter is to be wed soon."

"Yes. Condemned for the next forty years of her life. So innocent. Yesterday she pleaded with me again."

"Adil is a good boy."

"Javed is a good man." With a wave of her hand, "They all are."

"Javed has provided you with everything. Houses, cars, servants, more clothes than you can wear, jewellery others would gasp at. A position in society. Everything a woman would want."

Mona thought to herself but did not say, "…and we blame westerners for being materialistic." She simply said,

"Everything?"

Now Khadija was trembling. She crashed onto the sofa. "Get me some water, girl. Something is going to happen to me." Mona rushed to the kitchen and fetched a glass of water. Khadija drained it in one go. "More." Mona ran again, returning with another glass. Khadija drained it even faster than the first one. Puzzled and worried Mona asked, "More?"

"Yes. No. Yes. I mean sit down." Khadija was battering the sofa with her hand. Mona complied, still worried at Khadija's state. Slowly the elder lady composed herself. She was now completely calm and melancholic as if the water she drank was alcohol. Looking away from Mona, she exclaimed, "I loved someone."

"You!"

"I used to take great pains just to see him. Inventing reasons for mother to visit their house. To hear his manly voice." Turning to Mona, she said, "Haven't you noticed? I named my daughter Sabina after his first born." Mona was trying to figure out who she meant.

"That girl Sabina I met at your house on Eid."

"Yes, that Sabina."

"You love her so much. As a daughter."

"Yes."

"But her father… is… your first cousin."

"Now you got it."

"And you treat him like a… brother."

"With respect."

"But you still…"

"I love him still. Love is one thing we cannot control. I cook his favourite dishes. My husband isn't into food anyway. He eats any damn thing served. I watched all Dipal's movies because he looked like him. Not any more, of course. He has grown a pouch and lost his beautiful thick hair. But his voice is the same. His eyes are smaller. But they have the same intensity."

Mona felt sorry for her friend. "Khadija, all this time."

"I resolved if I could not have him, I would marry my child to his. But his son has turned out to be such a dope. He carries neither his father's looks nor his brains. He takes after his wretched mother."

"Have you…?"

"Told him?" With a chuckle, "He doesn't know. He was so good-looking. All us cousins were after him. I guess he lumped me with the rest. I never told him. Last year, when he had an accident and was in the hospital, how I wanted to be beside him. To help him. I couldn't."

"You are in pain."

"No. I am happy. He is safe. I get to see him on every family occasion. I have seen his life and know of all that happens in it. My daughter has grown up with his. The most important thing is not physical, though for a few years it was, but that he have a happy life. And that he has. I would have preferred it to have been me who brought him that happiness. But if we got what we wanted, we would be gods, wouldn't we?"

Holding Mona's hands in hers with their knees almost touching, Khadija continued in a softer tone. "Mona Ji. There is nothing wrong with loving another man. Love cannot be controlled. That is the beauty of love. But action can. Behaviour must be within norms set by society." With a whisper, she continued, "I have remained decent. And that is the call of the day for you."

Both friends looked away. After a long pause, Mona turned back to her friend. "Does he ever suspect or notice?"

Khadija smiled and with a tap on Mona's wrist said, "Girl, if men could notice, this would have been an entirely, entirely different world." They both laughed.

CHAPTER 15

Khadija ushered Mona into the room. "He is here," she said, and left. Mona walked sheepishly forward with her fingers locked in front. With slow, hesitant strides she approached Kamran.

"The weather…" she started, but then stopped, realising the futility of trying to hide the seriousness of their meeting. Kamran stood up, observing her carefully. His heart was beating as rapidly as a condemned man's before his execution. Mona saw his jawbone, his hands, his lean body. Then looked away, turned again and looked straight into his eyes. Her lips trembled. Eyes begged him for help. Kamran saw her beauty. All their meetings flashed in his mind. The awards ceremony, Kaghan valley. Her hair, her beautiful eyes. He saw the pain and knew what it meant. He said "You broke my heart. I will always love you," and left.

***

Mona slowly entered the garden. The workers were carrying away pieces of the large maple tree Javed had had cut down yesterday. She leaned on the wall, hidden from the workers. She must have been there for hours before Marina found her.

"What is the matter, Mama? I was looking for you. Why are you crying?"

"They cut the tree. It is gone. Finished," Mona said.

"But Mama, it was only a tree," Marina replied.

"You don't know, child. It is a lifeline. It links generations. Trees should be planted, not cut. We should be producers, not consumers."

She wept. Marina could not understand. "I'll be fine. Go inside. Watch some TV. Have your tea. Don't worry about me, Marina. I'll be fine."

***

Mona was still in the garden leaning against the wall. It had been hours since Kamran left, the workers left, Marina left. It was dark by now and Mona felt a chill but could not move.

A car pulled up and the driver rang the bell. From inside, a servant ran toward the gate. The driver asked him to inform Colonel Javed that Colonel Imtiaz was here to see him. Shortly after, Javed emerged with a hearty greeting and gave Imtiaz a big hug. Concealed by the wall, Mona could hear them. Javed invited Imtiaz into the house but Imtiaz refused. "This will be quick. I couldn't convey this over the phone. An Indian spy was caught crossing the border. After three days of intense interrogation, we managed to break the bugger. He said there is a high level mole in the Pak army. He didn't know the name but was certain the mole contacted Indian intelligence in Bangkok last month."

CHAPTER 16

The two buses struggled uphill on the meandering road leading to the hill station Bhurban. Muree used to be the attraction centre in these mountains, but ever since the five-star hotel was completed in the hillside, Bhurban became a popular destination. The passengers, girls from the arts college, were enjoying the scenery, tall pine trees and the valley beneath. Mona was calm and silent throughout the trip.

They finally arrived at the hotel. Looking at it from the front, the hotel seemed to be single story. At the check-in, though, Mona was told to take the elevator "down" to the third floor. The room was small but well-furnished. The bathroom was made of green marble and onyx. Mona opened the glass sliding door and stepped onto the balcony. She could see how the hotel wrapped itself along the contour of the mountain. Floors above her receded and the two floors below protruded, reminding her of the Spanish steps in Rome. The valley was deep below and small, scattered huts and wooden houses were engulfed in the thin descending cloud.

But Mona was not admiring this beauty. She paced the room before sitting down. She dialled a Rawalpindi number and told the operator she was calling from the PC Hotel in Bhurban. She wanted to speak with Colonel Javed. The operator asked who she was and Mona gave her name. The phone rang after a few minutes.

"Haven't you left yet?" Mona asked.

"I am running late. I am still at the Army Headquarters.

"I need to speak with you."

"Yes."

"Not on the phone."

Javed hesitated, then said, "I will be there in a couple of hours."

After a long nap, Mona walked along the trail. She found her party resting at a bend where the trail spread into a small enclave.

There were logs and benches. The girls were chatting. Mona sat on a bench and could see the valley below.

The girls had opened packets of chips, and the monkeys arrived. At first, they sat high in the trees observing, a constant chattering exchanged between them. Slowly, one braving the crowd descended its tree and walked up to Mona's bench, establishing his seat a couple of feet from her. He was old and seasoned. He made a shrill sound and looked at Mona. She dropped some chips, which he quickly grabbed and ran back up to his tree yelling instructions of encouragement to eyes and ears in the trees. Others descended, the younger, healthier ones first. Finally, mothers arrived with baby monkeys clinging to their backs.

Mona had just returned to her room when the doorbell rang.

"I came as fast as I could. I was with General Beg when you called," Javed said.

Motioning him to sit, she said, "I did not realize you were with Beg." Looking down, she continued, "I need to know what you are involved in."

Javed began casually, "My business ventures and property..."

Mona interrupted. "Why are you talking to the Indian intelligence? I know you met them on your trip to Bangkok."

Javed did not anticipate this and his shock was evident. He rose and gently took Mona's hand. Sliding the glass door, he walked onto the balcony. Mona followed.

"You see those mountains there. That is Kashmir. That is what we fight for. That is what we die for." Turning to Mona, with a soft voice he said, "I am a product of the army. From the son of a peasant to what I am today, I owe it all to the army. They trained me. Gave me a standing in our society. Let me assure you, I am loyal."

"You may be loyal to the army. But are you loyal to the nation?"

Javed did not expect this. He recoiled. After a moment's thought, he continued, "You obviously know more than is desirable. You know of my interactions with RAW? Do you know General Beg approved them?"

Mona was shocked. A sudden chill ran through her body. She went inside. Javed followed. "This world is not black and white. There is much grey," he insisted.

Mona was shivering, "Treason is not grey."

They sat in silence. Beg looked at Mona. He saw her long eyelashes. Her arms folded. She kept looking at the carpet. She looked so vulnerable. He shifted in the seat and began, "I need your support." After a pause, he went on. "I love you." Mona looked at his face then turned her eyes away. He continued, "I have everything yet I have nothing. Without you I have nothing." He sat on the edge of the seat. "What I do is for the family and the country. You must trust me." He held her hands.

"Do you think I like this life?" He looked toward the door. "Pretence, false bravado. Ultimate lies. Protect the country, my foot. We protect the land and sell the people. Hypocrisy."

"You seem to enjoy it."

Stiffening but then softening he replied, "I am a product of the system. Take me out and I will flourish. You mentioned Sufis. I went to Konya. I tried to understand but they make it so bloody confusing."

"Perhaps your effort needed more sincerity and depth," Mona replied.

He sat on his knees and continued, "England and France fought for 100 years. Now they are allies. Pakistan and India should be allies not enemies. Kashmiris would live in peace. Money could be diverted to social support programmes, to health and education for our people. We need allies to combat internal and external threats. Today Pakistan has a great threat from within –

fundamentalism. Trust me. Support me." He was exhausted and placed his head on her palms.

Mona slowly raised his head and looked into his eyes. He calmed down as if her calmness entered his body. She spoke with clarity and firmness.

"You will survive, Javed. We all do." With a sigh, she rose and left.

CHAPTER 17

The arrival of March ended the short spring in Islamabad. The heat had not yet caught up due to heavy rains. The big annual military parade was due in a few days and evidence of it was everywhere. Every day, roads were blocked for hours allowing military vehicles to transport their equipment and personnel. Barbed wire, military police and barricades were placed along the main boulevard, Jinnah Avenue, and most of its adjoining roads. Bus routes were altered. This was normal every year and the ordinary person in Islamabad considered it an unfortunate imposition.

The full-day rehearsal went well in spite of the drizzle. Organizers always dreaded March rain, which had a curious timing of coinciding with the day of the parade, the 23rd of March. The roads had been marked, police were stationed, and colourful canopies of the tents were set up on either side of Jinnah Avenue. Army technicians worked all week erecting the three VIP stands for military officials, foreign dignitaries and the chief guest. The chief guest podium was erected at the end of Jinnah Avenue, on the south side. This is where the top military brass would preside over the march past. To the north the beautiful lush green Margalla Hills, to the east the parliament building, and a little further down the white marble Supreme Court. The commentator's booth and TV cameras for the nine o'clock news were ready to capture the event.

Finally the day arrived. Military officers and their families were seated in VIP designated spots. A separate stand for dignitaries was occupied with foreigners from every embassy in the country. General Mushfi along with the chiefs of army, navy and air force was present in full military uniform. At nine o'clock the parade began.

It was an impressive sight. Unit after unit marched past the podium saluting the President in uniform. An armoured vehicle contingent displayed a variety of vehicle-mounted guns. There was a long procession of tanks followed by cannons, surface-to-air rocket launchers and armoured vehicles full of soldiers. Medium and long range rockets capable of carrying nuclear weapons were wheeled on large military trucks and received enthusiastic applause from the military stands. Air Force F-16 jets roared above, followed by helicopters from which a team of paratroopers bailed out. They carried the Pakistan flag. This was followed by the march of infantry units: the proud Baloch Regiment, the Punjab Regiment and the Sindh Regiment passed by in quick succession. Finally, the commando contingent arrived in their distinct camouflage uniforms. Armed with automatic weapons, they trotted more than marched. The energy was immense and the crowds roared with all eyes glued to the commandoes.

No one saw the lone gunman hiding in the thickest of Margalla Hills. He had taken his time assembling his gun and finding his target. As the commandoes approached, their leader, a fierce-looking man with a long black beard, raised his weapon above his shoulder and cried the war cry "Ya Ali!" His followers copied him. At that moment, the president, an ex-commando himself, rose to salute them. The leader of the commandoes raised his left hand and ordered his troops to halt. There was a moment of silence. One shot was fired. It echoed against the hills and sounded like a series of guns. The president hurled back over his chair and crashed behind the podium. He was dead before he hit the ground.

The commandoes encircled the chief guest podium and the military stands. Small arms fire broke out from some of the police and guards around the chiefs. The commandoes eliminated them with short bursts of automatic fire. Within minutes, the guards around the President and his chiefs were neutralised. There was pandemonium in the stands. Women were shrieking and running for cover.

A colonel flanked by two armed soldiers entered the news booth. Producing a script, he ordered the frightened newscaster to broadcast the following message: "By the grace of Allah, the Askari jihad has been successful. The rule of infidel General Mushfi has ended and the new age of Islamic government has begun."

***

Kamran sat in his apartment watching the news as events unfolded. The doorbell rang. It was Colonel Javed. "Do you remember me, Kamran Sahib?"

"Yes of course, Colonel Sahib. You lectured me on why we needed a strong military to counter the threat from India. Please come in."

"I still maintain strength is a virtue. But today we face a bigger threat – fundamentalism." He sat down and with a heavy sigh continued, "The Army is split down the middle, officers as well as soldiers. These are dire times indeed and the country needs your help."

"Only God can help this country."

"The enemy has taken over the command and control setup. They are within hours of controlling the nuclear weapons. We must act now."

"But my dear Colonel, isn't India the enemy?"

"This is no time to mock, Kamran Sahib. We must stop them and we need your expertise."

"But what can I do. I am only a civilian?"

"Encryption."

"What?"

"Your thesis. The algorithm you outlined in your thesis at Stanford."

"What do you know about that?"

"Everything."

Kamran sat down, turning his face away in disbelief. The Colonel continued, "The army adopted your algorithm for encryption. The chief security officer has joined the fundamentalists. They do not have the nuclear codes yet but will get them very soon. I can hook you into the central server. You must alter the code."

By now Kamran had recovered from his initial shock and was rather amused to know his work at University carried such value. He spoke with a tone of defiance, "Colonel Sahib. The army chiefs are under arrest. The coup is complete. There are pockets of resistance but these are too weak and I am afraid too late."

Now the Colonel gave a cunning smile "You underestimate the military. We have contingency plans. And we have powerful friends. This coup will fail and the secular forces in the military will prevail. Reinforcements have arrived."

"From where?"

"Across the border."

"Colonel, the Afghans are in no position to…"

"Not the Afghans."

"The Iranians would welcome a theocracy in Pakistan."

"Our Western neighbours cannot help."

Kamran's face turned pale. He could not believe what he was hearing. Slowly, he asked, "India?"

The Colonel nodded.

Kamran got up and walked away in no particular direction. Turning, he pointed a finger at Javed and blurted, "You want me to help the Indians defeat an Islamic revolution?"

"I want you to assist us, the secular military government, to defeat a fundamentalist revolt. India is merely supporting us as any secular government should. The secular forces will override the fundamentalists and regain control soon. In the meantime, we need you to alter the codes. The risks are too high and every possible precaution is necessary. You must buy us time."

"Either you lie or you have gone mad."

The Colonel sighed and returned to the door. Opening it halfway he beckoned someone in. A dignified gentleman wearing a three-piece suit entered. He was tall, well groomed, and approached Kamran with confidence. In a perfect Sandhurst accent he said, "Salam Kamran Sahib. I am Brigadier Srinath Singh of the Indian Army, covert operations."

"You are Indian intelligence -RAW?" Kamran asked in amazement.

After a quick glance at Javed, the brigadier nodded. Taking control of the situation, he motioned to Kamran. "Please sit down. There is no time to waste." He then waved to Javed, saying "Colonel Sahib."

All Kamran could utter was "I cannot believe this."

"Believe you must, Kamran Sahib. What is so surprising? Governments of two neighbouring countries working together. Isn't that how it should be?" Kamran did not answer. He kept his eyes on the brigadier, who continued, "You are well aware that the Pakistan senior military has close relations with foreign western powers. India is now a regional power. Instead of sole directions from the West, Pakistan now confers with Delhi on important matters. Just like the Moghul times."

"Has everybody sold out?"

"There are the diehards. Corps Commander Rawalpindi was not present at the march past. He was not captured. He held out till the rebels chopped his wife's finger off and sent it to him. He broke down and cried like a baby."

Kamran turned to Colonel Javed, who was now very nervous. "What has the military been offered?"

"Kamran, these are highly classified secrets."

"What is the deal?"

"The Indian units can fight the rebels. Our own Muslim units refuse to engage their brother Muslims. Think about it, Kamran. As allies, we would be invincible."

Kamran repeated his question with force. "What is the deal?"

Javed began to speak, but the brigadier interrupted him. "If the fundamentalists get hold of nuclear material, they are sure to use it. No sane person can be party to that." Standing up he spoke firmly. "Will you help us?"

Kamran nodded reluctantly. Swiftly, the brigadier pulled out a sheet with computer instructions and handed it to Kamran. "This would give you access to the server. I will call you in a couple of hours." He then moved to the far end of the room, pulled out his mobile phone, dialled and spoke with urgency. The Brigadier made three quick phone calls, each in a different language. Turning to Javed, "We must go."

Kamran began his work, quickly establishing an internet link with the military headquarters computers. After a couple of hours the phone rang. It was his dearest friend Zahid. He was frantic "What are you doing? They know."

"Who?"

"The Rebels. The Allies have scrambled aircraft."

Kamran assured him, "We don't need allies. All this country lacks is patriots."

"The Rebels have traced your location. Leave! Now!" The door smashed open. Armed men entered. Shots were fired. Within four hours, aircraft hovered over Kahuta, Chaman, Sargodha, Thatta and Chashma, cities with nuclear installations. Heavy bombs were dropped. The bombing lasted all night. Pakistan was no longer a nuclear state.

CHAPTER 18

The next day, the government announced the rebellion was defeated and the nuclear installations were intact. Western governments announced their support for the secular military rule with a cautious note that a plan for restoration of democracy was necessary and that an appropriate timeline for the withdrawal of foreign troops be adopted. The nation was in a state of shock.

On page three, the local newspaper reported a story of a man in Islamabad killed by burglars.

Made in the USA
Charleston, SC
27 November 2011